Everything in her responded to his kiss.

'I suppose you did that to—to take my mind off Steve,' Alison said, her voice far from steady.

There was a moment's silence. And then, to her consternation, Gavin threw back his head and laughed.

'My word, Alison, you do take yourself seriously!' he said, still very close to her. 'I kissed you for one reason only: because I wanted to. And what's more I enjoyed it, and I'm pretty sure you did too!'

Dear Reader

We travel again this month, to Spain and Australia in SWEET DECEIVER by Jenny Ashe, and OUTBACK DOCTOR by Elisabeth Scott. We also welcome back Elizabeth Fulton with CROSSMATCHED where American new broom Matt Dunnegan shakes up renal nurse Catherine, and Mary Bowring, who returns with more of her lovely vet stories in VETS IN OPPOSITION. Just the thing to curl up with by the fire as winter nights draw in! Enjoy. -

The Editor

Elisabeth Scott was born in Scotland, but has lived in South Africa for many years. Happily married, with four children and grandchildren, she has always been interested in reading and writing about medical instances. Her middle daughter is a midwifery sister, and is Elisabeth's consultant on both medical authenticity and on how nurses feel and react. Her daughter wishes she met more doctors like the ones her mother writes about!

Recent titles by the same author:

AND DARE TO DREAM
THE RELUCTANT HEART

OUTBACK DOCTOR

BY
ELISABETH SCOTT

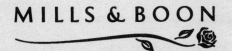

MILLS & BOON LIMITED
ETON HOUSE, 18–24 PARADISE ROAD
RICHMOND, SURREY, TW9 1SR

First published in Great Britain 1993
by Mills & Boon Limited

© Elisabeth Scott 1993

Australian copyright 1993
Philippine copyright 1993
This edition 1993

ISBN 0 263 78377 4

Set in 10 on 11½ pt Linotron Times
03-9311-55965

Typeset in Great Britain by Centracet, Cambridge
Made and printed in Great Britain

CHAPTER ONE

IT WAS the rain, that grey October day in Edinburgh, that made Alison decide to go home.

Home to the sunshine, the long dry months, the clear, unclouded sky.

Home to the vast distances, the far-off blue mountains of her father's sheep station in the outback.

Home to her folks, to the small dusty town, the hospital she knew so well, and old Dr Mac.

Home, most of all, to Steve.

She stood waiting for the lights to change, and she thought of how it would be, going home to Steve, telling him he was right, that she'd got the wanderlust out of her system, and all she wanted was to come home, and marry him.

She hurried across Princes Street, the soft Scottish rain on her face, just in time to catch the bus back to the hospital. Because now that she had made up her mind she wanted to get things moving right away.

Strange, she thought as she sat on the bus, how she had just known back there, suddenly and with complete certainty, that she didn't belong here. She loved Edinburgh, and she loved the huge bustling hospital — but it was time to go home.

'I don't believe it,' her friend Morag said, when they were having lunch together in the hospital cafeteria, three days later. 'You're going the day after tomorrow?'

'Too right I am,' said Alison, and took a notebook from her shoulder-bag. 'I didn't want to send a telegram to Steve until it was all arranged. I was fixed up to go on holiday this weekend anyway. And I'm due more leave, so Matron says she'll work a point for my notice. I've booked my flight, and tomorrow I'll send a telegram to my folks, and one to Steve.'

She showed Morag her notebook, with the two messages written out, ready to send. The one to her folks just said, 'Coming home Tuesday stop Steve will meet stop tell Matron I want job stop love Alison.'

The one to Steve said, 'Coming home stop you were right stop arriving some time Tuesday stop love Alison.'

Morag's blue eyes were concerned, as she gave Alison back her notebook.

'Alison,' she said slowly, 'I'm a wee bit worried. Oh, I knew about Steve, I knew he wanted you to marry him — but we've become good friends, you and I, in the time you've been here, and I've just never thought you were really missing him, or — or that you were madly in love with him.'

Her cheeks were pink, for she had a true Scottish reticence, a real reluctance to intrude on anyone's feelings. Alison thought, not for the first time, how much she would miss this girl.

'Oh, Morag,' she said, and smiled, 'we're not the sort of people to be "madly in love", Steve and I. I suppose we're both pretty sensible, practical people. As for missing him — well, I'm not one for wearing my heart on my sleeve, but more often than you'd think I've wished he were here, to share all this with me. You know yourself, all these dates you and Ian have set up for me — oh, I enjoyed going out, meeting people, but I always knew it would be Steve. And it just suddenly came to me, standing in Princes Street in the rain, that this wasn't right. I wanted to be back home in the outback, with him. Maybe that isn't too romantic, for someone who lights up the way you do any time she sees a certain doctor, but it's good enough for me, and it sure will be good enough for Steve.'

Steve had taken over his father's station, Borramunga, adjoining Blue Rock Ridge, Alison's father's station, a few years ago, when Alison had just started nursing in the small local hospital. She had loved her work there, loved living in the small dusty town of Namboola Creek, going home when she was off duty, seeing Steve, going to barbecues with him, riding over the vast plains.

'I suppose,' she said now to Morag, thinking about it, 'we both just thought we'd get married some time, without spelling it out.'

But it had only been when Steve suggested they should get married after the shearing was over, when he could get away from the station for a bit, that Alison's vague feelings had crystallised. Steve had been very understanding and undemanding, she thought now with compunction, when she'd told him she needed time first — time to see something more of the world than Namboola Creek and Brisbane. Sure, he'd been disappointed, but he hadn't tried to persuade her to change her mind.

All he'd said was, 'You'll find out that your place is here with me, Alison. But when you're good and ready, just say the word and come home. I'll be here waiting. Only thing is, I'm not much of a letter-writer.'

And that was true, Alison had often thought, especially in the last few months. Steve seemed to have kind of run out of things to say to her, and his letters had become shorter and shorter, more and more stilted.

'Maybe it was that,' she said now, as she and Morag took their cups of tea back to the table. 'That, and my mum breaking her wrist — she hasn't managed to write,

and my dad doesn't do much more than pass on news of
how things are going at Blue Rock Ridge, and how dry
everything is. I suppose I've been feeling kind of cut
off.'

'Homesick?' Morag suggested, warm sympathy in
her blue eyes.

'Maybe just a little,' Alison admitted. 'Anyway,
that's it. I just made up my mind, and I'm glad I can go
quickly.' She looked around the big, bustling cafeteria.
'I'll miss the hospital, and I'll miss Edinburgh. I love it
as much as I thought I would, hearing Dr Mac speak
about it. And for sure I'll miss you, Morag. But I'm
ready to go home.'

The last hours flew by, and she was glad of that,
because what she had said to Morag was true. She
would certainly miss the huge general hospital, and
working in Namboola Creek's small hospital would be
very different. But there would be dear old Dr Mac,
and Matron, and surely some of the staff who had been
there when she left, and it would be good to be back
there.

It was only when she was sitting in the plane, with
Heathrow and London falling away beneath her, that
she wondered, for the first time, if Steve would mind
that she'd told her folks to get in touch with Matron.
Maybe he'd wanted them to get married right away,
and she sure wouldn't be able to hold down a hospital
job when she and Steve were married, and living way
out at Borramunga. Besides, that was a job enough for
anyone, being married to a sheep farmer.

No, he would understand that she'd want to work for
a bit, while they got things fixed up.

I suppose we'll get engaged, and do the thing properly, she thought, drowsily, contentedly, leaning back
as the busyness of the last few days began to catch up

with her. We'll get engaged, Mum will get into the planning mode, she'll start making up lists, we'll have a trip into Brisbane to get a wedding dress, and Mum's outfit, and Dad will complain about the expense, but he'll be pleased that Steve and I are getting married.

The long, wearisome journey gave her plenty of time to think, because tired as she was, it just wasn't possible to sleep for long.

She could see Steve, the day she had left, his hat tipped back on his thick sun-bleached hair, his blue eyes crinkled in the brown of his face. His arms had been hard around her, as he held her close to him.

It would be good being back in Steve's arms again.

Good, too, to be back at home. That broken wrist of Mum's — she'd played it down, on the few telephone calls they'd had, but it had taken a long time to heal, and it couldn't have been easy, running the house, feeding the stockmen as well as the family. Meg, Alison's brother Brian's wife, would help, of course, but from what Alison gathered, with the baby on the way, Meg's morning sickness seemed to have gone on for a good part of the day.

That was something else that would be good, she thought, opening up her tray of food, and wondering how it was possible to feel hungry, when all you'd done was sit around for what already seemed like days — getting to know her sister-in-law. Brian and Meg had just got engaged when Alison left, and, although Meg's family had a store in the next town beyond Namboola Creek, Alison had only met her a few times. But she was an outback girl too, and Mum seemed to feel she'd settled down pretty well in their first year.

And, of course, Mum and Dad were thrilled about the baby. A grandchild, and a wedding, Alison thought — Mum will be in her element. And it probably won't be too long before Steve and I follow them. I've kept Steve waiting a fair bit; I guess he'll want us to go ahead and start a family as soon as possible.

The journey blurred into short snatches of sleep, more food, walking up and down the aisle to ease the stiffness. Perth, and then the long flight across Australia to Brisbane. Brisbane airport, waiting for her luggage, and then finding out about the flight to Namboola Creek.

She hadn't been able to give Steve a time for her arrival, because it had been beyond the powers of the travel agency in Edinburgh to find out about this last leg of her long flight, but she knew Steve would manage to find out. He'd know when she would arrive in Brisbane, and he'd know, too, that she would get the first flight possible after that. His cousin Pete worked for Landor Airlines, who flew into Namboola Creek; Pete would find out for him.

The tiny plane, after the huge jet, somehow seemed more like real flying. And it, Alison reminded herself, was bigger than the one they used from the hospital to reach patients in outlying districts in the Wet, when even the Land Rover couldn't get across the swollen and flooded rivers. As they drew nearer to the town, she looked out eagerly, identifying the untarred roads, the mulga trees lining the streets, the hospital at the far end.

The airstrip, and the big shed that served as waiting-room, offices, Arrival and Departure, were quiet today. She shaded her eyes against the remembered fierceness and clarity of the sunlight, and reached into her airways bag for her sunglasses.

There he was, her Steve, waiting at the door.

There were few formalities at this small airstrip, and

mostly folks just came right out to meet the passengers from the plane. But Steve didn't move.

Alison walked towards him, and when she reached him she dropped her airways bag and held out her arms.

'Steve — oh, Steve,' she said, not quite steadily. 'Gee, but it's good to see you.'

Afterwards, she thought that she had known, in that moment, that something was wrong, that something had changed.

Awkwardly he returned her hug, but when she lifted her lips to his he half turned, so that her kiss landed on his cheek.

Two years is quite a time, Alison told herself. And I did kind of spring it on him. And he always has been a bit shy in public.

She linked her arm through his as they went inside the shed.

'Bet I surprised you,' she said, 'just making up my mind like that.'

'Too right you did,' he agreed. He looked around. 'Let's have a cup of tea while they get the luggage off,' he suggested. 'You could do with one, after the flight from Brisbane.'

'I can wait,' Alison told him. 'Although maybe we should; it'll take us a good couple of hours to get home.'

He took her airways bag from her and carried it across to the two small tables that served as the refreshment area.

'I'll get the tea,' he said. 'Cloakroom's in the same place, if you want to freshen up a bit.'

It'll be fine, Alison told herself. We're just a little strange with each other, after all this time. Things will be better when we get out to the station.

And, she thought, looking in the mirror, when I get

some sunshine on my face. I probably even look different!

The girl in the mirror looked back at her, grey eyes questioning, thick brown hair framing her face. No freckles, Alison thought, inspecting her small straight nose. Not enough sunshine to give me any!

If she'd had time, she would have had her hair cut short before leaving Edinburgh, the way she'd always worn it, the way Steve would remember her. But I'll get that done soon, she decided; it'll be better in the heat.

Steve had poured tea, and he passed a thick white cup across the table to her.

'Good strong Australian tea,' Alison said with satisfaction. 'Great idea, having this first, Steve — I needed it more than I thought. Much too long to wait till we get to Blue Rock Ridge.'

Steve put his cup down. 'We're not going back right away, Alison,' he said. 'I have a message for you from the hospital.' He took a note from his pocket. Matron's handwriting.

Dear Sister Parr — Alison — I hate to do this to you, but Jean Butler — she's theatre sister now — has just had an emergency appendicectomy; we have Theatre scheduled for tomorrow, and there's no one I can ask. Thank heavens you're back! If you can give us tomorrow, I'll sort something out so that you can go and see your folks right after that.

Alison folded the note up and put it back in the envelope, a wave of relief washing over her. So that was why Steve was so strange. He was disappointed that she was to have to go right to the hospital.

'Nice to know I'm needed,' she said. 'So I'd better get right along to the hospital, get myself ready for tomorrow. Did you let my folks know, Steve?'

He nodded.

'Your mum says it's pretty crook, but she'll just have to wait a day longer.'

His blue eyes were still clouded, and there was none of the warmth she remembered in his smile.

'Steve,' she said, and put her hand over his, on the small table, 'it's only a day. We can wait. I know it's disappointing that I have to get right to the hospital, that we can't get into making plans or anything right away, but ——'

He drew his hand away from under hers.

'Alison,' he said, very steadily, 'there's something I have to say to you. I've been trying to say it for weeks, trying to tell you. Last week I wrote to you, but the day after I posted the letter your telegram came, saying you were coming back. And it was too late.'

The October day was hot, here in the outback, but all at once Alison felt cold.

'Too late for what, Steve?' she asked, and she hoped her voice was as steady as his.

'Too late for us,' Steve said quietly. 'I've met someone else, Alison.'

In all the years she had known him, she had never seen him look so troubled, so unhappy.

'I didn't mean it to happen,' he said, his voice low. 'I didn't want it to happen. I always thought it would be you and me, always thought you'd come back, as you said you would.'

And I did come back, Alison thought. But, as Steve just said, it was too late.

'Who is she?' she asked. 'Anyone I know?'

He shook his head.

'Her name is Tessa Cameron,' he said. 'She came here with her brother, a few months ago. She's ——'

I don't want to hear any more about her, not yet,

Alison thought. Carefully, deliberately, she finished her tea and put the cup back in its saucer.

'If you don't mind, Steve,' she said politely, 'I think I'd like to get right to the hospital — there must be things Matron wants to talk to me about.' She stood up.

'Alison, aren't you going to say anything?' Steve asked, a little desperately.

She had never known, until now, how very difficult it was to smile when your face felt as if it was frozen in place.

'What is there to say?' she said. 'We weren't engaged or anything, we just — just — had a sort of understanding. And now I'm the one who has to understand. And I will, Steve — I just need some time.'

When they were in his Land Rover, driving along the untarred road lined with mulga trees, he said, not looking at her, 'You came back, Alison. If you'd known this, maybe you wouldn't, maybe you would have stayed over there.'

Alison thought about that.

'Maybe I would,' she agreed, with honesty. 'But here I am, and it sounds as if they need me at the hospital.'

Neither of them said anything more, as Steve turned in the hospital gate and parked.

'I can manage,' Alison said, as he lifted her suitcase down. With difficulty, she smiled. 'You remember how strong I am!'

But with her hand in the handle of the suitcase she looked up at him.

'I'll be fine, Steve,' she told him, her voice steady. 'As I said, I — just need some time. Thanks for meeting me, and don't worry.'

She left her suitcase in the hall of the small nurses' home, and went across the hot and dusty yard to Matron's office, knowing only one thing. She could not—dared not—let herself think, yet, about what Steve had said. There was this obligation to Matron, to the hospital, and she was grateful for that. She was unbelievably tired, she realised, after the long journey, tired and stiff, and she would ring her folks, and then collapse.

Tomorrow would surely be a busy day in Theatre, and after that she would have to face up to all the implications of what Steve had said. Meanwhile, there was the reassuring familiarity of the hospital, of her work.

Matron wasn't in her office, and Alison had a moment of panic, knowing, with a certainty deeper than words, that she dared not let herself be alone, not yet. She needed to discuss work, to feel that this was where she should be. She decided to go along the corridor and say hello to Dr Mac.

His door was closed, but when she knocked her heart lifted with relief when she heard him say, 'Come in.'

She opened the door and went in.

'Dr Mac, I'm back, and——'

She stopped. It wasn't Dr Mac.

The man sitting at Dr Mac's desk was tall, with dark, untidy hair. His eyes were dark, in a lean sun-browned face. He was wearing a white coat, with an open-necked shirt under it. He was a complete stranger.

Alison looked at him, bewildered.

'Dr MacDonald only works one day a week now,' the man at the desk said. He stood up, and she could see that he was even taller than she had thought. 'I'm Dr Cameron, can I help you?'

He held out his hand, and Alison took it.

'Can I help you?' he said again.

'I suppose so,' Alison said, after a moment. 'I'm Alison Parr—Sister Parr—and I'm coming back to

work here. I got a message from Matron that I'm
needed right away for an emergency in Theatre.'

He looked down at her.

'Oh, yes,' he said, 'Sister Parr. Yes. I heard you were
coming back.' There was cool hostility in his voice now,
instead of the friendly warmth earlier.

It was only then that Alison realised. His name was
Dr Cameron. She stared at him, dismayed.

'You wouldn't make a good poker player, Sister
Parr,' the doctor said, and there was no amusement in
his voice. 'Yes, you're right. Tessa Cameron is my
sister.'

For once, Alison was at a loss for words.

Nothing and no one she had ever met before could
have prepared her for the hostility in Dr Cameron's
dark eyes as he looked down at her.

'And you, of course,' he said evenly, 'are the girl who
has kept Steve Winter on a string for years, and now,
just when he's found someone else, you've decided you
do want him.'

To her dismay, Alison found that her voice wasn't
quite steady.

'I—didn't know he'd found someone else,' she said,
with difficulty. And then, as the big, dark-haired man
looked at her, plainly unconvinced, a wave of anger
swept through her. She lifted her chin, and she could
feel her cheeks grow warm.

'I didn't know, until I landed here, that he had found
someone else,' she said, clearly, coolly.

Dr Cameron shrugged.

'Steve assured Tessa that he'd written to you,' he
said.

'He did, but I'd already left,' Alison replied. 'Not
that it's anything to do with anyone but Steve and me,
Dr Cameron.'

His hand gripped her wrist, so hard that it hurt.

'Get this clear, Sister Parr,' he said, his voice low. 'I will not have my sister hurt. If you think you can just come back, snap your fingers, and Steve Winter comes jumping, you'll have to think again.'

Alison pulled her wrist away and forced herself not to rub it where he had hurt her.

'I certainly don't intend hanging on to a man who doesn't want me,' she said. She knew, then and later, that she should have left it at that, but by now she was too angry to do that. 'But I've known Steve all my life, and I'd want to be very sure that he knows what he's doing. After all, a lonely man, here in the outback, not sure when the girl he'd asked to marry him was coming back——' The rest, she knew even as she said it, was unforgivable. 'He's fair game for anyone.'

For a moment, as Dr Cameron took a step towards her, she thought she had gone too far. And then, with an all too obvious effort, he controlled himself, and turned away.

'I would suggest that you see Steve and Tessa together before you make malicious remarks like that,' he said. 'And now, if you don't mind, I have work to do.' He sat down at the desk again.

For a moment, fuming, Alison stood looking at the bent dark head. But she knew she had already said too much, and she turned and went out, closing the door with exaggerated care.

And it was only then, as she stood in the hospital corridor with the closed door behind her, that she realised, with dismay, what she had just done.

She had undoubtedly made a bitter enemy of the doctor she was going to have to work with, the doctor who seemed to have taken Dr Mac's place.

The door to Matron's office was open, and Matron

looked up as she was about to pass, her plump, rosy face lighting up when she saw Alison.

'Alison, my dear,' she said, coming over and putting her arms around Alison. 'You don't know how glad I am to see you — oh, not just because we need you here, but I've missed you.'

Matron was an old friend of Alison's mother, and before Alison came to work at the hospital she had always been Aunty Trix, and both she and Alison had had to grow accustomed to a different relationship. By the time Alison went away, they had worked out an unspoken compromise, with the necessary formality in the hospital easing as soon as they were away from it.

But now it wasn't Matron's arms around her, it was Aunty Trix's, in spite of being in the hospital, and for a moment Alison clung to the comfort of that.

'I didn't know when you'd get in,' Matron said, stepping back to look at her. 'You look fine, but you could do with some sunshine.'

With an effort, Alison managed to hide her distress at her first meeting with Dr Cameron.

'I didn't know about Dr Mac,' she said, more abruptly than she had meant to. And then, with fairness, 'I suppose it happened around the time Mum broke her wrist, and it was ages before she could write, and even after she could her letters had to be much shorter.'

Matron's blue eyes clouded.

'He had to admit, finally, that he wasn't as young as he used to be,' she said. 'It was just too much for him. He comes in one day a week — he'll be so pleased to see you.'

'That's more than Dr Cameron was,' Alison said, before she could stop herself.

It was a moment before the older woman replied to that.

'Because of Steve and Tessa,' she said, and it wasn't a question.

Alison nodded, all at once not sure whether she could trust her voice.

'He — seems to think I heard about this girl, and came back because of that,' she said, with difficulty. 'But I didn't know until Steve met me at the airstrip.'

And then, because the older woman was part of her childhood, part of her growing-up years, she was able to say, still a little shakily, that she didn't want to talk about it right now.

'We have a busy day coming up tomorrow?' she asked, and she was grateful when Matron accepted the switch to something professional.

'Not too bad, but without Sister Butler we'd have had to cancel most of them. I can't work in Theatre now — my fingers are too stiff and arthritic. You'll enjoy working with Dr Cameron.'

I'm not so sure about that, Alison thought, remembering the way she and Dr Cameron had parted. But that subject was better left, for she had already been less than professional in even mentioning that Dr Cameron hadn't been too pleased to see her.

Instead, she asked about her room in the nurses' home.

'I don't know what you were used to in Edinburgh,' Matron told her, 'but nothing has changed here. There's always talk about upgrading the hospital, but I'll believe it when I see it. You'll be over to have something to eat, will you?'

Alison shook her head.

'I don't think so,' she said, for she was all too aware of how tired she was. Jet-lag, she told herself, on top of these last frantic days in Edinburgh. 'I just need to have a good night's sleep, then I'll feel human again.'

Matron sat down at her desk and reached for the telephone. 'Then I'll ask the kitchen to send you a tray with soup and toast,' she said briskly. 'In about an hour? That should give you time to bath. You'll be ringing home, of course.'

Alison nodded.

'Give Mary my love—I've already apologised to her for doing this to you,' Matron said. 'Come in tomorrow when you finish Theatre. You can borrow my utility to go home—it'll save anyone coming through for you.'

Although Alison had been away for two years, there was a reassuring familiarity about the small room. Even the curtains, she thought, were the same. Matron hadn't changed, and the hospital itself would be unchanged. And that, she knew even then, as she got into the bath, was what she would have to hold on to. The things that were familiar, and unchanged. Not anything or anyone different.

But that was dangerous ground, and she wasn't ready yet.

In her dressing-gown she went along the corridor to phone home. For a moment, as she was about to dial, she hesitated. It wouldn't be easy, talking to her mother.

'Alison? I've been waiting; I knew you'd ring as soon as you could—Trix feels bad about this, so do I, but surely the day after tomorrow you can come home?'

Alison's heart lifted at the warm familiarity of her mother's voice. She asked about her father, and Brian and Meg, about the horses and the dogs. And then there was no putting off any longer.

'You've seen Steve, of course,' her mother said

carefully. 'He said he'd be meeting you, and he said—'

'He told me,' Alison said quickly. 'Mum, I—haven't really taken it in yet, I need time to think about it.'

'It must have been quite a shock,' her mother said, after a moment, and her voice was still careful.

Alison thought of Steve's letters, over the past weeks. Looking back, she knew that she should have seen there was something wrong—but that was easy enough now, with hindsight.

'How do you feel about it, love?' her mother asked, and the warm sympathy in her voice was almost too much for Alison.

'We'll talk about it when I get home,' she said.

'We'll do that,' her mother agreed. 'Now you get yourself off to bed, and have a good night's sleep, girl.'

'I'll do that,' Alison promised. 'Give my love to Dad, and Brian and Meg.'

The tray of tea and toast arrived soon after she got back to her room, and as soon as she had finished she got into bed. The heat of the day was beginning to ease, and already the steady distant hum of the small hospital was familiar and reassuring. She could feel her eyelids becoming heavier and heavier.

Early as it was when her alarm woke her, the sun was already streaming into the small room. With the ease of long practice, Alison washed, dressed, had some scrambled egg, tea and toast, and hurried across the compound to the hospital.

The theatre was small, for patients needing more specialised surgery were sent to Brisbane, or to Charleville. She studied the list, relieved to find that it wasn't a long one. Two tonsillectomies, one appendicectomy, and some minor surgical procedures. And I suppose, she thought, as she checked the autoclave, and the sterile packs, an ingrowing toenail can be pretty uncomfortable!

It was some time since she'd worked in Theatre, and she was glad that she had time to check everything, time to remind herself of her role, especially here, where there would be only herself and the doctor. No anaesthetist, no scrub nurse.

She was in her theatre gown when she heard the door open. Dr Cameron came in, throwing off his shirt as he strode through to the small changing-room. Alison had a momentary and disconcerting glimpse of a brown chest, before she turned away quickly and re-checked the sterile tray she had already checked.

'Morning, Sister,' he said, from inside the room. 'Everything ready?'

'Yes, Dr Cameron,' Alison replied, as he came out of the room, turning his back to her so that she could tie his theatre gown.

'Thanks for stepping in at such short notice,' he said, and his voice was completely professional, as he began scrubbing up.

Alison was glad that she didn't have to reply, for just then their first patient arrived. Young Molly Barton, who had just finished her training when Alison went away, wheeled the trolley in. Her freckled face lit up when she saw Alison, and she mouthed, See you later, as she and Alison transferred the drowsy patient, a boy of seven, to the operating table.

As Molly left, Alison opened a sterile pack and held out gloves for Dr Cameron to put on. Then his mask, and then her own scurbbing and mask and gloves.

'Feeling good and sleepy, Glen?' the doctor asked the boy, his voice muffled by the green mask. 'Now, remember what I told you yesterday, about counting?

Right after I give you this little jab—right, that's it—you're going to start counting. Right, then.'

'One, two, three, four—five—six. . .' The boy's voice tailed off.

Alison put the sterile drape in position, and Dr Cameron nodded, his eyes meeting hers for a moment.

'I've been putting off doing this little fellow,' he said, as he worked. 'I always hope kids will outgrow tonsil troubles, but there was severe hypertrophy, and the pharynx was occluded, and the airway endangered.'

He held out his hand, and she handed him the scalpel.

'By rights, he should have been done in Charleville, by the ENT man, but the waiting list is miles long, so we do the fairly straightforward ones here,' he added.

Alison wasn't sure, afterwards, if he was determined to rescue their professional relationship and separate it completely from the disastrous meeting of the day before. If that was what he intended, it worked, for she found herself absorbed by her own part, and by watching his surgical skill.

The time flew by, with only a brief snatched tea break, and the ingrowing toenail had just been removed when Matron herself appeared at the door of the theatre.

'Dr Cameron, we've got an emergency—one of the stockmen from Borramunga with a fish-hook in his hand. Says he was fishing in the dam a couple of days ago, and he thought the hook would come out on its own.'

The stockman, his weatherbeaten face white under the tan, held out his hand silently when Molly brought him through, as soon as the toenail patient had been wheeled out.

'Look at this,' the doctor said, and pointed to a thin

red line running up the man's arm. 'The infection's spread to the lymphatic system — we'll have to keep you in for a couple of days, have you on antibiotics, and keep an eye on this. Maybe next time you'll have more sense.'

The man nodded.

'Guess I will, Doc,' he agreed. 'Just go ahead and do it — I feel pretty crook right now.'

Alison scrubbed up again while Dr Cameron anaesthetised the stockman, and by the time he himself had scrubbed up she had swabbed the man's hand and draped a sterile towel around it.

'I'll have to extend the entry wound,' the doctor murmured, more to himself than to her. She handed him the scalpel she thought he would need, and after his slight nod had told her she was right she watched as he extended the wound, and carefully extracted the fish-hook. Alison passed him a swab, and he cleaned the deepened wound.

'That should do it,' he said at last. 'I'm not stitching completely, I want to leave a drain in — yes, that small one — in case there's any more poison.'

When he had finished, Alison bandaged the man's hand.

'Can you get hold of Nurse Barton, Sister?' the doctor said, throwing his rubber gloves into the disposal bag. 'He can be taken back to the ward now.'

'Yes, Doctor, I'll phone right away,' Alison replied.

'Not here, you won't,' Dr Cameron said. 'You're not in a big hospital now, you're back in Namboola Creek.'

Annoyed at herself, Alison said stiffly that she would go along to the ward and let Nurse Barton know. As she reached the door, Dr Cameron called her back.

'Do you mind untying me, Sister? I never can reach these darn things.'

Alison undid the ties of his theatre gown.

'Thanks, Sister,' he said. And then, 'You've done a fair bit of theatre work, I can see.'

It was, she realised, a compliment.

'Yes, I have,' she replied, and she knew her voice was still stiff, knew that her own focus on their purely professional relationship, which she had been conscious of as they worked together, was gone. He was, once again, the man who had accused her of coming back here because she couldn't bear the thought of Steve falling for someone else.

He looked down at her. For a moment she thought he was going to say something else, but he turned away abruptly, his lean face dark, closed.

Alison was to have two days off, Matron said, and said, too, that she wished it could be more, but with Jean Butler still off they were even more short-staffed than usual.

'But I've put you on the afternoon shift, the day you start again,' she said. 'You can have two nights at home, and drive through in the morning.'

She gave Alison the keys of her utility, insisting that she didn't need it for the next few days.

'I hear you were very efficient in Theatre today,' she said as Alison was leaving. 'Gavin Cameron was most impressed.'

Gavin. So that was his name.

'He's a good surgeon,' she replied, a little unwillingly.

That night Alison went over to the dining-room. Like her room in the nurses' home, it hadn't changed, and she said so to Molly Barton, sitting down beside the younger girl when she had collected her plate of stew and vegetables.

'Neither has the food,' Molly pointed out ruefully.

'Great to have you back, Alison. It must be quite a change for you — Edinburgh, you were working in, were you?'

Alison nodded.

'That's what I want to do,' Molly said wistfully. 'Have a couple of years either there, or in London, take the chance to have holidays on the Continent. There's a course in paediatric nursing I'm keen on — do you know anything about it?'

'Yes, I know a couple of girls who did it,' Alison told her. 'I'll get them to send you details, if you like.'

Molly's face lit up.

'Gosh, thanks, Alison, that'd be great. But once I get over there I'm not sure that I'd want to come back.' She stopped. 'Oh,' she said flatly, and her face flamed.

Yes, Alison thought. It's still a mighty small world in Namboola Creek. There can't be many folks who don't know that Alison Parr came back all set to marry Steve Winter, only to find he didn't want her, he'd found someone else.

Unconsciously defiant, she lifted her chin. It wasn't going to be easy, meeting people she knew, seeing not only interest, but pity, in their eyes.

'I'm sorry, Alison,' Molly said now, awkwardly. 'I wasn't thinking — I mean — '

Somehow Alison managed to smile.

'Don't worry, Molly,' she said, as lightly as she could. 'I guess I'm going to have to get used to that sort of thing.'

She finished her meal, wondering if she was just imagining that the half-dozen or so folks in the dining-room were talking about her, were speculating about how she was feeling.

She stood up. 'I'm off early tomorrow morning,' she

told Molly. 'I think I'll go and make sure I've got everything ready. See you.'

She walked across the compound, grateful for the slight coolness that came with evening. The day's work in the theatre had kept her too busy to think, too occupied to allow her to begin to examine how she felt about what had happened. But now, alone, she couldn't put it off any longer.

The girl who had stood in the rain in Edinburgh and decided that she was coming home to marry Steve — that girl, confident and happy, sure of herself, sure of Steve — seemed very distant from the way Alison felt now.

She knew that she was dangerously close to tears, and she was determined that she wasn't going to cry. Not here, not now.

There was a light in the room that had been Dr Mac's. Dr Cameron must be there, late as it was.

It's all his fault, Alison thought, knowing, deep in her heart, that she was being illogical and unfair. It's all his fault, for coming here to Namboola Creek, and bringing his precious sister with him!

CHAPTER TWO

ALISON left the hospital early the next morning, while it was still fresh and cool. And somehow, in spite of all that had happened to change this homecoming, her heart lifted when she drew out of Namboola Creek and headed towards home.

Slowly and surely, the haze of the distant mountains, the vastness of the plains, and the clear, unclouded blue sky, brought some peace and some comfort. Here, at least, nothing had changed.

There was hardly any water in the river, and it was no problem for the sturdy vehicle she was driving to take it. Later, when the rains came, and the river was really flowing, it could be different. But that could be some time. Last year the rains had been poor. Born and brought up on the station, Alison looked at the brown, dry scrubland, and knew that many of the farmers must be getting worried. Not much feeding there. And always the danger of a bush fire.

Once she was over the river, she always felt she was almost home, for although it was still fifty miles to the homestead, all the land she could see on this side of the river belonged to Blue Rock Ridge. As children, and as they were growing up, Alison and Brian had ridden all over the vast station with their father.

She drew up outside the house, as her mother came out on to the wide and shady veranda, carring a tray of tea.

'Saw your dust miles away, and I knew you'd be good

and ready for tea,' she said, as Alison got out of the utility.

Her words, and her voice, were brisk and matter-of-fact, but her arms were warm and welcoming, and it was so good to be home again, where she belonged, that Alison, who regarded herself as just as brisk and practical as her mother, was taken aback to find herself close to tears.

The wildly enthusiastic greeting from their two dogs, now honourably retired from being working dogs to enjoy living in the house, gave her a chance to recover.

'Too right, I need that tea,' she said quickly, sitting down on one of the comfortable cane chairs. 'How's your hand, Mum?'

Mary Parr held out her brown right hand.

'Much better,' she said. 'But it does get a bit stiff sometimes — a touch of arthritis set in, Dr Mac says. Never mind me, though.' She looked at Alison, her brown head — with more grey than there had been two years ago, Alison saw with a pang — tilted to one side. 'So much for all the Scottish high teas — you're as thin as ever.'

'You're just jealous, Mum,' Alison said comfortably, 'because I'm like Dad — we can eat anything, and we do, and never put on an ounce.'

Her mother put her teacup down, and her blue eyes were clouded.

'Alison, love,' she said, not quite steadily, 'we knew when your telegram came that you hadn't heard from Steve. He rang, right away, and told us he'd written, but too late.'

Too late. Yes, that was what Steve had said.

'He should have written sooner, to tell you,' Mary Parr said now, her cheeks pink. 'He said he would, but — it wasn't easy. I suppose he just kept putting it off. I do blame him for that.'

Alison looked at her mother.

'But not for anything else?' she asked carefully.

Her mother's hand was warm, covering her own on the table.

'Alison, folks have to follow their hearts,' she said. 'There's nothing your dad and I would have liked more than to have you marry Steve, and live on the next station. But you went away, and you didn't make any promises to Steve.'

'No, I didn't,' Alison agreed, her voice low. And then, the words bursting out of her aching heart, she said, 'But he said he'd wait, Mum; he said when I was good and ready just to come home, and he'd be waiting.'

'It's a long time, two years, love,' Mary Parr pointed out.

Alison looked away, towards the distant blue hills that gave the station its name, but her eyes were blurred with tears.

'Too long for Steve, certainly,' she agreed, not quite steadily. She wiped the back of her hand across her eyes, annoyed with herself, for she always prided herself on not being the crying sort.

'Here's Meg,' she said, with relief, seeing her sister-in-law coming across from the cottage where she and Brian lived. 'Meg, you look as if you could have this baby any time,' she smiled, hurrying to meet the girl coming up the steps.

Meg's cheek was warm against her own as they kissed.

'I know,' she agreed cheerfully. 'I keep asking if it's twins, because I'm only due in a month, but look at me!' She took the cup of tea her mother-in-law had poured for her. 'Thanks, Mum. Glad to have you back to do your aunty stuff, Alison. I'm sorry things haven't worked out for you and Steve. It must have been quite a shock.'

'Yes, it was,' Alison replied, grateful for Meg's straightforward approach.

As they sat and talked, and she answered Meg's questions about Edinburgh, about the hospital, she knew, with relief, that she was going to get on well with Brian's wife.

'Where are Dad and Brian?' she asked.

'Checking out the fencing beside the dam,' her mother said. 'One of the stockmen thinks he saw a dingo in after the sheep. They'll be back pretty soon.'

It was late afternoon before Jim Parr and Brian came home, and by then Alison had been to the stables, greeted Sultan, the chestnut she usually rode, and been shown around the cottage by Meg, all the time accompanied by the dogs.

She was grateful for the matter-of-fact approach from her father and her brother too.

'Silly young fool,' her father said gruffly. 'But I will say this for him, he came and spoke to us straight. Pity he put off doing the same for you.'

'Maybe as well he didn't,' Brian said. 'Maybe you wouldn't have come back if you'd known, and Meg and me are mighty glad to have you here, aren't we, Meg?'

'Too right we are,' Meg agreed. She patted her bulge. 'This little fellow here can be the man in your life for a bit, Alison.'

'Meg's sure it's a boy,' Brian said, and he smiled across the table at his wife.

'Did you have a scan?' Alison asked.

Meg shook her brown curly head.

'I could have, if I'd gone to Charleville,' she said. 'But Gavin Cameron looks after me just fine.'

'Most folks in Namboola Creek seem to think pretty well of him,' Mary Parr commented. 'And Trix is pretty impressed. What did you think, working with him, Alison?'

'He's a good surgeon, I'll grant you that,' Alison said, right away. 'But as for what I think of him personally — I've never met a man so insufferably rude, so — so arrogant!'

There was a surprised silence around the table.

'So you didn't exactly take to him, I gather?' Brian said after a moment, deadpan.

Reluctantly Alison joined in her family's laughter.

'You always did jump in and make your mind up too quickly,' Mary Parr said. 'How on earth can you know Gavin Cameron well enough to be so certain? For goodness' sake, Alison, give the man a chance!'

He didn't give me much of a chance, Alison thought. He made up his mind about me before he even met me.

She stood up. 'I'm not wasting my precious time at home talking about that man,' she said briskly. 'Meg, I guess you're not interested in an early ride these days — what about you, Brian?'

'Sure,' her brother agreed. 'Meet you in the stables at six — Meg will have breakfast ready for us when we get back. All right, love?'

'Barefoot, pregnant, and in the kitchen, that's how he likes me,' Meg said, but her eyes met her husband's, and Alison could see the warmth and the strength of the love between them. And for a moment her heart turned over. It could have been like that for Steve and me, she thought.

It was like old times, the next morning, she thought, as she and Brian splashed through the river-bed on horseback. Over the plain then, and towards the distant hills, pink-tinged in the early morning. They ended up on the hill that overlooked the house, both of them breathless, and then they raced down and towards the stables, Brian only just winning.

Meg had prepared a traditional Australian breakfast of steaks topped by fried eggs, one for Alison and herself, two for Brian. At last, after two mugs of tea, Brian left them, and Alison helped Meg to clear up.

They talked, the two girls, about the coming baby, about Meg's family, about the plans to extend the cottage.

'You're lucky, you and Brian,' Alison said slowly.

Meg looked at her. 'I know that,' she said, her voice low.

Alison hesitated, but only for a moment. 'What's she like, Meg, this girl?'

Meg's hazel eyes met hers steadily. 'She's very different from you,' she said, after a moment. 'She's small, fair-haired, blue eyes. Pretty—yes, she's pretty. A quiet girl, and she has a—I don't know, a fragile look about her.'

Alison looked at her, not bothering to hide her dismay.

'She doesn't sound much like the sort of wife for a man who runs a sheep station the size of Borramunga,' she said, more brusquely than she had meant to.

It was a moment before Meg replied.

'I don't suppose she does,' she agreed. 'But——' she looked at Alison, and now her eyes were troubled '—I don't want to hurt you by saying this, Alison, but you'll see for yourself, sooner or later. The way Steve looks at her, the way they look at each other—maybe she isn't the right sort of girl to live on a sheep station, but I don't think that bothers Steve one little bit. I'd say that they're pretty gone on each other.'

Unbidden, there was the memory of Gavin Cameron saying to her that she should see Steve and his sister together before she made — what had he said? — malicious remarks. Alison felt her cheeks grow uncomfortably warm.

But he was the one who got nasty first, she reminded herself quickly, and a healthy anger replaced the momentary embarrassment.

Meg was looking at her curiously.

'Are you all right, Alison? I didn't mean to upset you, but I think it's only fair to — kind of warn you. I mean, I wouldn't want you thinking this isn't the real thing, because I'm pretty sure it is.'

Alison assured her sister-in-law, not entirely truth-fully, that she wasn't upset, and then, with complete truth, that she really was glad to know what Meg thought about Steve and this girl.

Then, whistling to the two dogs, she went off for a long walk.

It was hot already, and soon she was forced to walk more slowly. By the time she reached the bend of the river, behind the house, she was glad to sit down in the shade of a mulga tree. The dogs lay beside her, panting.

Maybe Meg's wrong, she thought. Maybe Steve's just kind of dazzled by someone so different, here in the outback. What was that old song Mum used to sing? 'Bewitched, Bothered and Bewildered'. Maybe that was what it was, just as she'd said to Gavin Cameron — Steve, lonely for her, and all right, maybe she shouldn't have used words like 'fair game', but when you got right down to it that was what she thought.

She stood up. No, Dr Gavin Cameron, I certainly won't hang on to a man who doesn't want me, she thought. But, as I said, I'd want to be very sure he knows what he's doing!

She stood up, and turned back towards the house, the dogs at her heels, and her head held high.

In spite of everything, Alison was glad to be back at the hospital the next day.

She took Matron's keys back to her, along with some jam her mother had sent, and asked which ward she was to be on.

'I've just been talking to Dr Cameron,' Matron said, and if she noticed an immediate stiffening from Alison she ignored it. 'You're going to be most use on Maternity—that's where most of your experience has been, these last few months in Edinburgh, I gather, and that's certainly where we need you here. If there's any emergency for Theatre before Jean Butler's back at work, we'll make some arrangement for you to assist Dr Cameron, but there's nothing urgent for next week, so he's postponed his list. Jean should be back by the next week.' She stood up. 'I'll take you along to the ward now. Young Molly Barton has just been transferred from General—she's young, but you'll find she's keen.'

The maternity ward had only six beds in it, and at the moment two were empty. Three of the women had already had their babies. Alison was pleased to recognise Hazel Shaw, who had been a year above her at school.

'Your first, Hazel?' she asked, admiring the two-day-old baby boy feeding hungrily.

'My third,' the dark-haired young woman told her. She held her baby closer. 'But Tim's got his boy now, so that's it. Don't you think he's like Tim, Alison—sorry, Sister Parr?'

Alison looked at the tiny red-faced scrap, and thought of Tim Shaw, a big, fair-haired man who now owned one of the local garages. She looked again at the baby.

'Well, maybe about the eyes——' she began cautiously.

The young mother smiled.

'All right,' she said cheerfully. 'But Tim and his folks think he's the dead spit of Tim, so we're all happy!'

The other mother was the wife of a stockman on one of the more distant stations, and her baby was slightly jaundiced.

'But he's much better now, Sister; he was like a little Chinaman the first day,' the young mother told her. 'Dr Cameron says another day should do it, then I can go home.'

The other new mother, Alison saw from the chart, had diabetes, and, although her baby was already four days old, she was to stay for further observation.

She checked the last patient, who was in the early stages of labour, and took the charts back to the duty-room, which served as an office too, to study them, leaving Molly in the ward.

All pretty straightforward, she thought, but the diabetes woman would have to be watched. She carried the chart over to the window, to read the doctor's instructions.

'Four-hourly temps, in case of sepsis, graduated exercise,' she murmured, nodding as she read aloud. 'And ambulant, to minimise the risk of thrombo-embolism.'

'You're happy with my orders, Sister?'

She turned round, warm colour flooding her cheeks, at Dr Cameron's voice.

'Oh — of course, Doctor,' she replied, furious that he should see her at a loss.

He picked up the other charts, and then, after a moment, put them down.

'I believe you were home for a couple of days?' he asked.

A little surprised, Alison said that yes, she had been.

'How's Meg?' he asked.

'She's all right,' Alison answered, a little surprised at this lack of formality.

'Still sure it's a boy?' Gavin Cameron asked.

'Very sure,' Alison told him.

To her further surprise, the doctor smiled.

'I have a bet with her that it's a girl,' he said. 'What do you think?'

'I don't know,' Alison replied, rather at a loss, for she hadn't expected Dr Cameron to talk to her like this, after their first disastrous encounter.

She turned to go back to the ward, but before she reached the door the doctor's voice stopped her.

'Sister Parr,' he said. Alison turned round. 'I owe you an apology,' he said, with some difficulty. She stood still, unable to say anything. 'I talked to Steve,' he said abruptly, as if, she thought later, he just had to get this over with. 'He told me that his letter to you was too late to reach you. I — I jumped to conclusions, and I was wrong. I'm sorry.'

It wasn't, Alison thought later, that she was trying to be difficult. She was just so taken aback that she didn't know what to say.

'For goodness' sake, woman,' he said, so loudly that Alison was sure the whole ward would hear, 'you might at least say something!'

Alison took a deep breath.

'I'm glad you know that,' she said, and that was true.

'But you didn't give me much of a chance, did you? You were all too ready to believe the worst of me.'

Unbidden, then, there was the memory of her mother telling her so many times, through the years, that she herself was too ready to make her mind up quickly about people, one way or the other.

Gavin Cameron took a step towards her. His eyes were very dark as he looked down at her. Alison was suddenly, and most disconcertingly, aware of him not as the doctor she would be working with, but as a man. To her chagrin, her heart thudded unsteadily, and she could feel slow, warm colour rising in her cheeks.

And then, just as abruptly, Gavin Cameron turned away.

'You could do with learning to take an apology gracefully, Sister,' he said, and his voice was once again completely formal. He was, once again, the doctor, and she was once again the sister. The strange and disturbing moment was over, and Alison tried to tell herself that she had imagined it.

'I'm sorry, Doctor,' she returned, just as formally. 'And now, if you don't mind, I have to get back to the ward.'

As she walked along the corridor, she thought, It's all very well, him saying he's sorry. But that doesn't change anything, as far as Steve and I are concerned.

Steve and I. The words echoed emptily in her mind.

For it was no longer 'Steve and I', as far as she was concerned. And, most of all, as far as Steve was concerned.

But Alison wasn't prepared to set aside the thoughts she had had the day before, sitting beside the river. She owed it to Steve, and she owed it to herself, to be quite certain that he knew what he was doing.

*   *   *

As the familiar routine of the small hospital claimed Alison again, sometimes it seemed to her that she had never been away, that the two years in the large and bustling hospital in Edinburgh had been only a dream.

But then something would bring her up short, and remind her that it was no dream, that she really had been away. And that so much had changed in that time.

Hurrying to fill in charts before she went off duty, she would find herself thinking that it wouldn't matter if she was a little late, Steve would understand. Because there had been so many times, in her years of nursing here, when she had hurried off duty, breathless, to find Steve waiting for her, to hear his slow, easy voice telling her it was all right, when she apologised for being late.

But not any more. Now, when she went off duty, there was no one waiting for her. And Steve would be with someone else.

And again, in the ward, checking the beds and the lockers and making sure the patients were all not only comfortable but tidy as well, before it was time for the doctor's round, she would find herself thrown when it wasn't Dr Mac, with his silver head and his comfortable stoutness, coming in.

But as the days went by, gradually she became accustomed to the knowledge that there would be no Steve waiting for her, and accustomed to seeing Gavin Cameron come in to the ward each morning, his white coat flying, his thick dark hair usually rumpled.

And slowly, unwillingly, she came to admit that he was a good doctor. He was efficient, and he was thorough, but he was much more than that. Seeing his hands, big and brown and somehow both gentle and reassuring at the same time, as he examined a patient, Alison knew that he was a caring doctor.

Since his somewhat brusque apology to her — and,

she had to admit, her undoubtedly ungracious acceptance of it—she was able to maintain their professional
relationship without always thinking of that first disastrous meeting.

But, to her annoyance, she found it less easy to forget
that strange moment when he had moved close to her,
and his dark eyes had looked down at her, and she had
been suddenly and disturbingly aware of him as a man.

'He's a honey,' young Molly Barton said brightly,
one morning, when Gavin Cameron had just left the
ward.

In spite of herself, Alison had to smile. A honey? It
seemed a most inappropriate word for this big dark
doctor.

'Well, you must admit he's good-looking,' Molly
insisted.

'Good-looking? No, his face is too strong for that,'
Alison said, thinking about this. 'He's too—rugged,
really, to be called good-looking.'

'One thing's for sure,' Molly said, handing Alison a
mug of coffee, 'he's the most interesting man to have
hit Namboola Creek in a long time!'

Alison put her mug down on the desk.

'Sure,' she agreed. 'But I'll stick to someone like
Patrick Swayze, rather than Dr Cameron!'

The telephone rang then, and it was the station
manager from Quincomba, about sixty miles away, to
say he was bringing his wife in right away.

'And this time she says she means business,' he said.

This was the young woman who had been in on
Alison's first day. It had turned out to be a false alarm,
and she had gone home.

'Could be quite quick, now that she's started,' Alison
said, checking Linda Hutton's file. 'Her due date was
two days ago—Dr Cameron said if nothing had hap-

pened in a few days we'd have her in anyway. Molly, check the delivery trolley, and I'll go across and tell Dr Cameron.'

Gavin Cameron was with Matron when Alison found him, drinking coffee.

'Like Drake and his game of bowls, time to finish this, and do a quick round of the general ward,' he said. 'See you in the labour ward, Sister.'

Labour ward, Alison thought as she checked the small room, was a very kind term, if you were to compare it with the labour ward she had worked in in Edinburgh. One bed, a drip, an incubator. Not that that should be needed for this baby; the mother's last check-up showed a big and healthy baby, and full-term now.

Dave Hutton must have driven mighty fast, she thought when the Land Rover screeched to a halt outside the maternity ward, and the big, red-haired man helped his wife out.

'She reckons there's no time to lose,' he said, as Alison hurried to meet them.

Not much wonder, after a drive like that, Alison thought, as she assessed the young mother's contractions, before doing an internal examination.

'Go and get Dr Cameron,' she said to Molly. But she could see that this baby was on the point of being born, so she eased her fingers into the tight rubber of the gloves.

'I should have come in sooner, but I was afraid it was a false alarm again,' Linda Hutton said. Her forehead was damp, and Alison signed to her husband to wipe it, as another strong contraction brought a gasp from the young mother.

'So you're not fooling us this time?' Gavin Cameron

asked, coming into the room and over to the bed. For a moment, his eyes met Alison's, and he nodded.

The baby's head was showing.

'Go ahead, Sister, you're all ready to deliver,' he said.

After that, there was no time to waste. Gently Alison eased the baby's head out, and then, with a sudden slippery movement, the shoulders followed, and the baby was born.

'A boy, and he has his father's red hair, Linda!' Gavin Cameron said.

Molly was there now, ready to take the baby, and Alison returned her attention to her patient, waiting for the contraction that would deliver the placenta. Only when she had cleaned up her patient could she turn again to have a look at the baby, but she had heard a few reassuringly loud cries, and now, when Molly put the baby boy into his mother's arms, the tiny mouth was already eagerly seeking his mother's breast.

'Knows what to do right away, this one,' Dave Hutton said, and his big hand gently touched the baby's cheek. 'You did a good job, Linda, girl.'

Alison peeled off her rubber gloves.

'You did a good job too, Sister Parr,' Gavin Cameron told her.

His words were formal, but there was a warmth she had never seen before in his eyes. Professional appreciation, Alison told herself, but in spite of that she couldn't help feeling a glow of pleasure.

'It was a very straightforward delivery, Dr Cameron,' she said.

'I know,' he agreed. He smiled. 'I look forward to seeing you do one that's more of a challenge.'

He turned then to the young parents, and, just as the

father had done, he too touched the baby's cheek, without saying anything.

Alison, as a very young pupil midwife, had decided that there were two kinds of doctor. There were those who looked on childbirth as just another aspect of their work, to be done efficiently and professionally. And there were those who saw each birth as a small miracle. She had the strange and disturbing certainty now that Gavin Cameron fell into the latter category.

He looked up and saw her watching him.

'This little fellow's good and healthy, isn't he?' he said, trying to hide, Alison thought, half amused and half annoyed, his reaction to the baby.

Molly brought cups of tea for the new mother and father, and Gavin Cameron raised his eyebrows.

'No tea for me, because I was too late to do the delivery?' he asked.

Alison coloured. 'I'll make you some in the duty-room,' she said. 'Nurse Barton, you can check that Mrs Hutton's bed is ready.'

'But——' the young nurse began, but Alison drew her out of the room.

'I know it's all ready, Nurse,' she said. 'But let's give those two a little while on their own, with their baby.'

'Oh—oh, of course, Sister,' Molly said, her cheeks pink.

'Nice touch, Sister,' Gavin Cameron commented, following her through to the duty-room.

Alison switched the kettle on.

'Well, they're not going to have much privacy when Mrs Hutton is in the maternity ward,' she said. 'And it's a very special time.'

'Yes, it is,' Gavin Cameron agreed. 'Though I wouldn't have——' He stopped.

Alison handed him a cup of tea, trying to control the slow, burning anger she could feel rising inside her.

'You wouldn't have thought I'd be capable of such an unselfish thought?' she asked, and she was glad that her voice was steady.

'I'm sorry,' the doctor said. 'I shouldn't have said that.' He finished his tea, and put his cup down. 'Thanks for the tea, Sister,' he said. And then, unexpectedly, he sat down on the edge of the desk. 'You haven't seen Steve since the day you came back,' he said, and it wasn't a question.

'No, I haven't,' Alison replied. 'I — don't think there's anything to be gained by Steve and me seeing each other, at the moment.'

He looked at her, and she could see that he was considering the wisdom of saying anything more.

'Don't you think,' he said, quite gently, 'that you might find it easier to accept the situation if you were to see Steve, talk to him? And, even more, to see Tessa and him together.'

Alison stood up.

'I've accepted the situation, as you call it, Dr Cameron,' she said, knowing as she said it that this was not entirely true. 'And I really don't see that there's anything to be gained by seeing Steve or your sister. I've put the whole thing behind me, and I don't want to waste time thinking about it.'

His eyes were very dark, and very steady, as they held hers. And Alison, very conscious of her determination to be sure that Steve knew what he was doing, looked away.

'I don't think you're being entirely honest with yourself,' Gavin Cameron said. And then, his lean brown face, taut, and any gentleness or warmth gone, 'Or with me.'

Without another word, he left the room.

And Alison, holding on to the saving anger she had felt towards this man, was all too conscious, as well, that she wasn't going to find it too easy to forget that strange and disturbing and different aspect of him which she had seen when the baby was born.

It was Matron who insisted that Alison had to go to the barbecue in the school grounds.

Dr Mac had already spoken about it, when he was in the hospital for his one day a week, but when Alison said she wouldn't be going the old man hadn't pressed her but had only said again, gruffly, that he was glad to have her back.

But Matron wasn't to be put off as easily as the old doctor.

'It's a fund-raiser for the hospital,' she reminded Alison. 'For the things the government says they can't afford to provide. New curtains, some rugs in the waiting-room. Reverend Jones says if there's enough money we need a fish-tank, so that folks will feel more relaxed. No, Alison, we've all got to put in an appearance, and you're not on duty.'

Alison thought of all the townsfolk who would be there, and her heart sank. So many people she'd known all her life looking at her, talking about her, feeling sorry for her.

'Can't I switch duties — let someone go who really wants to?' she asked, a little desperately.

But Matron shook her head.

And so, on the night of the barbecue, Alison changed out of her uniform, and put on jeans and a T-shirt. Then, with decision, she took off the T-shirt and pulled out a shirt she'd bought in Edinburgh a few weeks before she left. The shirt was silky, and her favourite greeny blue, and when she had brushed her hair and put some clear coral lipstick on she looked at herself in the mirror in her room.

There was defiance in the tilt of her head, she knew, but she knew, too, that the colour of the shirt made her hair more russet than brown, and did something good for her grey eyes.

'All right, Namboola Creek, here I come!' she said, and she went out of her room, head held high, to the compound. Tim Shaw from the garage was to use his big Land Rover to take people along the road to the school grounds, but there was no sign of it.

I could walk, Alison thought, but as she reached the hospital gate a Land Rover drew up beside her.

'Get in — I'm sure we're going to the same place,' Gavin Cameron said.

Alison shook her head. 'I can walk,' she said.

'I'm sure you can,' the doctor agreed pleasantly. 'But there's no need to, when I'm going there too.' And then, his voice impatient, he said, 'For goodness' sake, get in — this is ridiculous.'

Silently Alison climbed in. 'Thank you,' she said stiffly.

Gavin Cameron turned to her.

'Doesn't Namboola Creek pride itself on being matey?' he said. 'And won't folk think it's pretty funny if you and I are so formal? So let's bury the hatchet, at least for tonight — Alison.'

It was a moment before she replied.

'All right,' she said, knowing she sounded as grudging as she felt.

The doctor was waiting.

'All right — Gavin,' she said.

On the short drive up the dusty, untarred main road, he asked her about the hospital in Edinburgh. A little unwillingly at first, Alison began to talk. But his genuine interest made it easy to bring out her thoughts and impressions of the huge hospital.

'It must have been quite a culture shock working there, after our little place here,' he said, and although it was dark she could tell from his voice that he was smiling.

'Too right it was,' she agreed. 'It was pretty exhausting, but a real challenge, all the time, to keep on top of things.'

Gavin swung the Land Rover into the school grounds. Ahead of them, there were lights strung up, and the noise and bustle of the barbecue.

'Some time,' he said, turning to her, 'I'd like to hear about Edinburgh. My grandparents came out from there — I've always wanted to go to Scotland.'

'Yes, I knew you must have a Scottish background,' Alison said, and she was glad of the darkness, to hide the sudden colour in her cheeks at the realisation that her words said all too clearly that she had certainly thought about him.

The doctor was already out of the Land Rover, and round to her side, but she jumped down before he reached her. He made no comment, though, but instead, as they walked towards the lights, he said that he thought it must have been his Scottish name that made old Dr Mac think he was the man for the job.

They were close to the crowd of people now, and unconsciously Alison braced herself.

'You'll do fine,' Gavin Cameron said quietly.

Startled, she looked at him.

'There's Hazel Shaw,' he said. 'And that looks like pretty good steaks she's handing out.'

Soon, a little bewildered, Alison found herself with a plate in her hand, a large steak on it, and a long table of salads, rolls and baked potatoes ahead of her. She spoke to Hazel Shaw about her baby, and then Matron — Aunty Trix, now that she was away from the hospital — called her over to talk to Jean Butler, almost recovered from her emergency appendicectomy, and insisting she would be back to work in a day or two.

'Though I hear you did pretty well standing in,' she said cheerfully. 'Maybe I should think about retiring.'

Gavin Cameron was further over, talking to the station manager from Bindoota. He raised a hand, and Alison waved back, conscious yet again of the confusion of emotions this man could make her feel. Always, underlying everything, there was the resentment for the way he had judged her before he even met her. But right now she knew that he had gone out of his way to help her to face up to coming here tonight.

Because now that she was here it was all right. Oh, she knew there were one or two curious glances, but mostly the folks she knew were making it as easy as possible for her; no one had mentioned Steve's name, and she was grateful for that.

And then, as she was talking to Jean Butler, she was conscious that the older woman's face had become suddenly still, that she was looking over Alison's shoulder towards the gate.

Alison turned round, knowing that what she had half expected, and certainly dreaded, had happened. And she didn't think, now, that she could handle this.

Steve stood there, his eyes searching the crowd. But Alison had eyes only for the girl beside him, the girl his arm was protectively sheltering.

She was small and slim, as Meg had said, and her iong fair hair was loose on her shoulder. Pretty — my word, yes, Alison thought, she was pretty, this girl.

As Alison watched, the girl said something to Steve, and he bent closer to her, smiling.

No, Alison thought, no, I can't take this. I don't have to. Blindly she turned away. But before she could head for the kitchen, or the Ladies', or anywhere, Gavin Cameron was beside her, his hand on her arm.

'Come and meet my sister, Alison,' he said, quite loudly, and she could see that everyone near by had heard him.

'No, I——' she began, but his hand tightened on her arm, like a vice.

'Stop scowling,' he said, his voice so low that she was the only one who could hear it. 'Smile, and look pleasant. And try to look as if you don't give a damn!'

CHAPTER THREE

'I CAN'T,' Alison said, her voice as low as his. 'Let me go!'

'Yes, you can,' Gavin Cameron told her.

His hand was firm and unrelenting on her elbow as he led her across to Steve, and the fair-haired girl beside him.

'Hi, Steve — Tessa,' he said cheerfully. 'Alison, I'd like you to meet my sister Tessa. Tessa gave up the bright lights of Canberra to come and keep me company here.'

Tessa Cameron's eyes were such a deep blue that they were almost violet. Her hand was small, and it was shaking, Alison realised with surprise, when she held out her own hand to the other girl. Surprise, and an emotion that could not possibly, she told herself, be pity. Pity, for the girl who had taken Steve from her?

'Tessa,' Gavin said.

He looked, Alison thought, like a parent whose child hadn't said please or thank you at a party.

'Oh — oh, yes. I've been wanting to meet you, Alison,' Tessa said shyly.

I bet, Alison thought, and now the strange and disconcerting feeling had gone.

'And I'm glad to meet you,' she replied politely. And perfectly truthfully. Because all her doubts were confirmed. How in all the world did Steve expect a girl like this to fit in and help him run Borramunga?

Somehow this confirmation of her doubts gave her back her confidence. That, and the realisation that people around them were either tactfully turning away, or just weren't interested, now that they had seen that Alison Parr and Tessa Cameron had met, with no fireworks on either side.

'How've you been, Steve?' she asked pleasantly.

Steve coloured. 'Fine,' he answered awkwardly. 'How about you, Alison?'

'Oh, you know me — an outback girl born and bred. I'm just so glad to be back home.' She paused. 'Whatever,' she added deliberately.

For a moment, a tide of colour flooded Tessa Cameron's face, and then drained away, leaving her eyes huge in the small white face. And Alison, in spite of her own hurt, was ashamed of herself.

Gavin took a protective step closer to his sister, and once again there was hostility in his dark eyes as he looked steadily at Alison for one long moment.

'How are your classes going, Tessa?' he asked.

'Fine, Gavin,' Tessa replied. 'I've got three new pupils in the last couple of days.' She turned to Alison. 'Sometimes when Gavin's late at the hospital we don't connect,' she explained. 'Especially now that I have one or two classes in the evening.'

'Classes?' Alison asked, knowing she should try to make amends for the way she had spoken.

'I teach dancing,' Tessa told her. 'Ballet and modern, and I've just started an aerobics class.'

'Dancing classes here in Namboola Creek?' Alison asked, astonished. 'And aerobics?'

Tessa Cameron flushed.

'Why not?' she said, her small pointed chin raised. 'Most little girls would love the chance to learn ballet.' She paused, and her violet eyes met Alison's. 'Even little girls in the outback! And you'd be surprised how many young women—and older—are interested in modern dancing, and in aerobics.'

Unwillingly, Alison had to admire the girl's show of spirit. But she had had enough now of standing here smiling, talking to Steve and this girl. Not that Steve had said a great deal; he probably found the whole situation too embarrassing.

'Alison and I were on our way to dance,' Gavin said then, smoothly and unexpectedly. 'See you later.'

This time, as they walked away, his arm was around her shoulders, casually. Casually, but firmly.

Without asking her, he led her on to the small wooden platform set up for dancing. The music was loud, and the dance-floor was crowded, making any conversation impossible, but his arm held her close to him. Unnecessarily close, Alison thought, her face warm, and she tried to draw back.

Gavin's arms tightened around her, and she could feel his breath against her hair.

'Just relax, and try to look as if you're enjoying yourself,' he murmured, his mouth close enough to her ear to let her hear. 'You've done not too badly up to now—just keep it up. I suppose it was too much to expect you to be all sweetness and light.'

'You don't have to hold me quite so tightly; I'm not going to run away,' Alison returned, deciding to ignore the last remark.

'I'm not so sure about that,' the doctor said.

Steve and Tessa were dancing now as well, Tessa's fair head close to Steve's. The music, from being loud and fast, had changed to something slow and dreamy, and it looked, Alison found herself thinking, as if these two were in a world of their own, close together, their arms around each other.

A feeling of loss and desolation swept over her, and

she missed a step. Gavin looked down at her, questioning. She turned away, but she knew he had seen the expression on her face.

'Let's go and have something to eat,' he said. 'I could do with a cup of coffee, and I saw the minister's wife setting out some super-looking pavlovas.'

It was easier with her back to the dance-floor, Alison found, and it had been unexpectedly thoughtful of Gavin to bring her away. Especially, she had to admit, after the way he had looked at her when she made that remark about being glad to be back in the outback, whatever.

Somehow the rest of the evening passed. There were so many people to talk to that after that she only saw Gavin in the distance, sometimes with Steve and Tessa, but more often with other groups of people. Once she saw him with Dr Mac for a long time, the old doctor and the young one talking, sometimes seriously, sometimes both of them laughing.

'The new doctor seems to have settled in well, really become part of the place,' the minister's wife remarked when Alison was helping her clear away coffee-cups. 'Thanks, dear, we're not doing any washing up tonight, unless we need more cups. Oh—we were just talking about you, Gavin.'

'Were you, now?' Gavin Cameron murmured, and there was amusement in his dark eyes as he looked from the older woman to Alison. 'Alison, I'm heading back for the hospital—I'll give you a lift.'

He does take things for granted, Alison thought resentfully.

'I don't——' she began.

The doctor shook his head.

'I know you're on duty at seven tomorrow,' he said.

'I'm sure you must be ready to go back now. Why do you always have to argue?'

All too conscious of Mrs Jones's interest in this conversation, Alison decided it would be easier to give in.

'You didn't have to take me back just because you gave me a lift along here,' she said as she climbed into the Land Rover.

'That's one of those things I like about you,' Gavin replied; 'always so grateful when anyone does anything for you!'

Unwillingly, Alison had to smile. In the moonlight that lit up the cab, he looked down at her.

'You look much better when you smile, you know,' he said, quite softly.

'So do you,' Alison said, before she could stop herself.

Gavin shook his head.

'You always have an answer, don't you?' he said.

He started the engine and drove out of the school grounds, and back down the street to the hospital. But, instead of driving across to the brightly lit door of the nurses' home, he stopped at the other side, where it was dark.

'Thanks for the lift, I'll just ——' Alison began hastily.

'Oh, no, you won't, not just yet,' Gavin said. Then his arms were around her, imprisoning her. Then, with one hand, he traced the outline of her mouth, in the darkness of the cab. This is ridiculous, and I should move away right now, Alison thought hazily. But the touch of his finger on her lips did strange things to her, and she was conscious of her heart thudding unevenly, as she wondered how it would feel if he were to kiss her. Knowing, even as she wondered, that he would.

His lips were gentle at first, gentle and searching.

And then, quite suddenly, demanding, and his arms holding her close to him. And she had no more thought of breaking away, for everything in her responded to his kiss, to his touch.

Later — much later — they drew apart. And, free from the bewildering and unexpected closeness, Alison could feel her face warm with colour, at the way her body had responded to his.

Now she drew back.

'I suppose you did that to — to take my mind off Steve,' she said, furious to find her voice was far from steady.

There was a moment's silence. And then, to her consternation, Gavin threw back his head and laughed.

'My word, Alison, you do take yourself seriously!' he said. He was still very close to her, and it just wasn't possible to move further away. 'I kissed you for one reason only: because I wanted to. And what's more I enjoyed it, and I'm pretty sure you did too!'

Arrogant, impossible man, Alison thought furiously.

But there was no way she could deny her response to him, and she didn't try to.

Without another word, and with as much dignity as possible, which wasn't a great deal, she climbed out of the Land Rover cab and walked across to the brightly lit door of the nurses' home. Conscious, all the time, that Gavin Cameron was watching her.

There was only one thing for it, she told herself the next day, as the time approached for Gavin's round, and that was to be as cool and as professional as possible.

It wasn't, after all, the first time she'd been kissed by a doctor she was working with. She thought of the good-looking houseman in her training hospital in Brisbane, and the sluice cupboard that was his favourite place for pouncing on young nurses. And there had been that Irish doctor in Edinburgh, and the nice young registrar when she was on Casualty.

Oh, no, Dr Cameron, she told herself, you're certainly not the first doctor I've kissed and had to face the next day!

For a moment there was the memory of the way she had felt in his arms, the knowledge that she had never felt like that before.

But why not? she asked herself, sensibly and reasonably. He's a—an attractive man, after all, we were alone, and I was in a fairly emotional state. So it isn't really surprising, the whole thing.

But that didn't make any difference, of course, to the cool and professional way Sister Parr would greet Dr Cameron when he came to do his rounds.

'Morning, Sister Parr—sorry I'm late,' Gavin said, hurrying in, his white coat, as always, flying open, his thick dark hair a little untidy. 'Right, just as well we have only a couple of patients here—they're completely full over in General.'

No doctor, Alison thought a little later, when he had gone, could have been more cool, more professional. And of course that was just how she would want him to be.

'Dr Cameron didn't waste much time, did he?' Molly said, a little wistfully. 'I was still busy bathing the babies, and he just came in, had a quick look at both of them, and he was off again.'

She looked at Alison under her lashes.

'Must have been nice, dancing with him,' she said. 'Is he a good dancer?'

'Difficult to tell,' Alison replied, quite truthfully. 'There wasn't enough space for real dancing.'

But unbidden, then, there was the memory of

Gavin's arms around her as they danced, holding her close to him.

'We have some time in hand, Molly, I'd like to check the supplies cupboard,' she said briskly. 'Looks as if by next week we could be a lot busier.'

When they had finished, Alison took her checklist across to Matron's office. Matron wasn't there, and Alison went along the corridor to look for her, thinking that perhaps she was in the general ward.

But as she passed Gavin Cameron's office he beckoned to her, before turning back to the desk where the two-way radio was set up.

'I've just tuned in for emergency calls—got the Blue Rock Ridge sign,' he said briefly. 'Hang on, they're coming in now.'

Meg, Alison thought. But it was at least a fortnight early. Still, you could never tell with babies.

'Five minutes apart? You're certain? No, Meg, you can't do that, there won't be time. You'd never make it through here.' For a moment, his eyes met Alison's. 'I'll get Rick Garrett to bring me. Tell Brian to be at the airstrip to meet me.'

He signed off then and turned to Alison.

'You heard that? Right, we need to get moving. I'd like you to come with me.'

The hospital had an arrangement with Rick Garrett, who ran the small hotel, that his small plane would be available when it was needed. The doctor lifted the phone and got hold of Rick Garrett's wife.

'Blue Rock Ridge,' he said. 'And I want to leave immediately.' He turned back to Alison. 'We'll take the portable incubator,' he said. 'It shouldn't be needed, the baby should be big enough, but I'd rather have it.' He looked at his watch. 'Be back here in five minutes, Sister, ready to go.'

And then, unexpectedly, his briskness was gone, and his hand covered hers for a moment.

'She'll be all right, Alison,' he said. 'With luck, we'll get there in time, and if we don't your mother is there.'

There was no time to think, no time to do anything but hurry back to her ward, tell Molly what was happening, and collect the antenatal and the postnatal packs, always kept ready for an emergency such as this.

And it did happen from time to time, Alison reminded herself, as she sat beside Gavin, heading, very fast, for the airstrip. Most of the stations were pretty distant from Namboola Creek, and although usually women came in to town a few weeks early, and stayed with relatives or friends, sometimes there wasn't time for that.

Like now.

Only this time it was her brother's baby, the first grandchild for her parents.

Rick Garrett was already at the plane, waiting, when they reached the airstrip.

'I'll have you there in half an hour,' he shouted, against the noise of the propellers.

Soon Namboola Creek was beneath them, like a toy town, and they were heading towards the river. And from this height, even with her tearing anxiety for Meg and the baby, Alison could see how brown and dusty everything was, and how low all the dams were.

The tiny airstrip at Blue Rock Ridge was about a mile from the homestead, and before they landed Alison could see the Land Rover there. Her father was at the wheel, and as soon as Gavin and Alison ran over he started the engine and headed for the homestead.

'How's Meg?' Alison asked.

'Brian and Mum are with her,' her father said. 'She

hasn't long to go, I'm pretty sure; I just hope we're in time.'

'If we're not, it won't be the first baby born before the doctor gets there,' Gavin pointed out. 'And I'm sure Mary is able to deliver her own grandchild if necessary.'

But in spite of his reassuring words he was first out of the Land Rover the moment it stopped outside the house.

Mary Parr was at the door. 'Through here, Gavin. Alison, I was hoping you'd be here too, and so is Meg.'

Meg was sitting on the bed, and Brian had just sponged her forehead.

'Thank goodness you're here,' he said, when they went in. 'I've delivered quite a few calves, but I sure didn't want to have to deliver my own baby!'

He stood back, while Alison opened the antenatal pack and handed Gavin rubber gloves. Swiftly, expertly, he examined the girl on the bed, stopping when a strong contraction made her draw in her breath and bite her lip.

'You're doing fine, Meg,' he said. And to Alison, 'She's fully dilated, going into second stage any minute. You staying with us, Brian?'

'Sure,' Brian replied. 'As long as I'm not in the way. Meg says I'm good at the back-rubbing.'

But he did look a little white, Alison thought affectionately, as she and her mother worked together to get the bed ready for the delivery.

'How will I know when I want to push?' Meg asked, and her voice was a little wobbly.

It was her mother-in-law who answered. 'You'll know, girl,' she said briefly.

And a few moments later Meg gave one outraged gasp and said, 'I want to push now.'

'Right, Meg. Alison will give you a whiff of the mask here, just to keep you more comfortable.'

When Alison removed the mask, Gavin said to her, his voice low, 'You want to do the delivery, Alison?'

Alison shook her head. 'No, thanks,' she said emphatically. 'I'm too close to this baby.'

And a moment later she was so glad that Gavin was there, that he was in charge. For as the baby's head crowned, and then appeared, she and the doctor saw, at the same time, the cord around the tiny neck.

'Hold everything, Meg,' Gavin said, in a voice that brooked no argument. 'Don't push, pant like a dog.'

Meg said afterwards that she knew by Gavin's voice that something was wrong. Alison took her hands and told her, over and over again, not to push. Brian, Alison saw fleetingly, was even whiter. Gavin's dark head was bent as he worked, carefully and swiftly, to free the baby's neck.

'All right, Meg, push now,' he said. And Alison knew by his voice that everything was all right, that he had managed to cut the cord before there was any harm done to the baby.

'One more push, and you'll have your baby,' she said to Meg, and the next moment the little body appeared. Gavin handed the baby to Alison, waiting with the receiving blanket. A couple of surprisingly healthy yells reassured her right away of the healthy state of the baby's lungs.

'Well, well, Meg, I win my bet,' Gavin said, and Alison knew the triumph in his voice was not for that, but only for the safe delivery after what could have been so different. 'You've got a little girl!'

Alison handed the baby, wrapped in the blanket, to her sister-in-law.

'A girl?' Meg said, taken aback. 'Are you sure?'

For a moment, Gavin's dark eyes met Alison's in shared amusement.

'Oh, yes,' he assured her gravely, 'I'm sure. I have had some experience in this sort of thing.'

Gently, wonderingly, Meg touched the tiny face.

'A little girl,' she murmured wonderingly. 'Well, what do you know? Brian, isn't she beautiful?'

Alison looked at the tiny red-faced scrap in her sister-in-law's arms. Better-looking than most newly born babies, she thought, but beautiful? And she marvelled once again at the miracle that made every new baby beautiful to its mother.

'Tea,' her mother said briskly from the door a little later, when Alison had cleaned Meg up and helped her into a fresh nightie. 'I reckon we all need it, not just you, Meg. But the rest of us are going through to the kitchen to have it.'

She poured tea for Meg and for Brian, and handed it to them.

The pilot was waiting in the kitchen, drinking tea, when they went through. Gavin sat down at the kitchen table beside him, and took the mug of strong tea Mary Parr handed to him.

Across the table, Alison looked at him. If he hadn't been there, she thought soberly, Meg and Brian could have lost their baby.

'Don't look so serious, Alison,' Gavin said, looking up. 'Everything's fine.'

'It might not have been, though,' Alison said. And then, without giving herself time to think, she said what she had been thinking. 'I'm glad you were here, Gavin.'

It was a moment before he replied.

'So am I,' he said quietly.

And she had the strange feeling that he wasn't

thinking only about the baby he had just safely delivered.

With the drama and the tension of the baby's birth behind them, everyone in the kitchen at Blue Rock Ridge seemed to feel light-hearted. Especially, Alison thought in some surprise, the doctor.

Gavin and the pilot, Rick Garrett, swapped flying stories—Gavin had worked with the Flying Doctor service for a short time—and Alison, laughing at an improbable story of Gavin's about a plane bogged down in a river-bed, and a couple of inquisitive kangaroos, found her mother's eyes resting on her thoughtfully. She coloured, knowing very well that her mother was remembering what she had said about this man.

Arrogant, and insufferably rude.

Well, so he can be, Alison reminded herself. He just happens to be different—right now.

'I should bath the baby,' she said, rising with a reluctance that surprised herself.

Gavin rose too.

'Think we've given Meg long enough to bond with the little girl she was so sure would be a son?' he asked.

'I should think she's already forgotten she ever thought it would be a boy,' Mary Parr said, smiling. 'Alison, Dad went over and got the baby's bath from the cottage—I'll get it ready, looks as if there's everything you'd need here. Come on, you men, take your tea outside—we need this table.'

Meg was leaning back against her pillow, the baby cradled in her arms. She looked tired, but there was that indefinable glow about her that Alison had seen on so many new mothers. And Brian was obviously on top of the world.

'I wanted a daughter right from the start,' he said,

when Gavin and Alison went in. 'We can have a boy next time.'

Gavin smiled down at Alison.

'Next time,' he said. 'They're already talking about next time, and this child doesn't even have a name!'

'Oh, yes, she does,' Meg told him. She kissed the top of her baby's head. 'She's going to be Ruth Alison.'

Absurdly, Alison felt her eyes fill with tears. Gently she took the baby from her sister-in-law.

'I want to see her being bathed,' Meg said. 'Brian, hand me that dressing-gown of your mum's, please.'

Brian looked at her.

'Are you sure?' he said doubtfully. 'Shouldn't you stay in bed for a bit?'

Meg shook her brown head.

'I've had a baby, that's all,' she said. 'Right, Alison?'

'All right with me,' Alison said.

'And with me,' Gavin said. 'As long as Aunty Alison doesn't mind an audience for the bathing?'

There was warm laughter in his voice, and in his eyes, as Alison replied that she didn't mind at all.

He really is a strange man, she thought, confused and more than a little thrown by yet another side to the doctor she had dismissed as arrogant and insufferably rude. I don't know where I am with him. Aunty Alison, indeed!

And in spite of herself it was difficult not to smile at the way he had said it.

The audience consisted of the proud parents, the even prouder grandparents, and the doctor, as Alison showed Meg how to look after the cord, then expertly soaped the tiny body, and then dipped little Ruth Alison into the warm water. Mary Parr had laid out the smallest clothes she could find for the baby to wear, and soon Alison held out a pink and sweet-smelling baby to her mother.

Meg held her baby daughter close for a moment.

'Will you hold her, please, Mum?' she said to her mother-in-law. 'I'd like to phone and tell my folks. But before I do—surely there's no need for me to go through to Namboola Creek, to the hospital? I mean, what's the point in that, now that I've had the baby?'

Gavin shrugged.

'All right with me,' he agreed. 'You've got help here—you can radio for any advice you need—and I'm sure Alison will be back as soon as possible to check on everything. I'd like you to come through in a couple of weeks, let me have a look at you and at the baby, though.'

Mary Parr looked up from her absorption with her baby granddaughter, and suggested to Meg that she should ask her mother to come and stay for a bit.

'Your dad, too, if he can get away,' she said. 'But your mum will be wanting to see the baby right away, spend some time with her. I could use the help, too.'

Half an hour later, when Jim Parr drove Gavin and Alison, and the pilot, back to the landing-strip, it was all settled. Meg's folks were to drive through the next day, but her father would go back right away. And Mary Parr, when she had hugged Alison and said goodbye, held out her hand to the big doctor.

'Thanks for everything, Gavin,' she said. 'Look, why don't you come out for a weekend some time? Maybe next time Alison's coming home, if it fits with your time off——'

'Thanks, Mary, I'd like that,' Gavin said. And then, casually, 'If that's all right with you, Alison?'

'Oh—oh, yes, of course,' Alison replied, thrown by her mother's unexpected invitation to the doctor, and all too conscious of the colour in her cheeks. Because there was something disturbing, somehow, in seeing Gavin Cameron here in her home, and she had a strong conviction that it wouldn't be a good idea to repeat this. She wished, with all her heart, that her mother had at least spoken to her first before doing that. But, knowing her mother's warm hospitality, added to her gratitude for what Gavin had done today, she was pretty sure any objection she could have made would have been over-ruled. But it would have been helpful not to have it sprung on her like that!

The flight back seemed to take less time, with the anxiety about Meg and the baby gone. Back at the airstrip at Namboola Creek, Alison and Gavin collected the Land Rover, and put the antenatal and postnatal packs into the back. And the portable incubator.

'Thank goodness we didn't need that,' Gavin said. 'I was pretty sure the baby was big enough, and she was, after all, only a fortnight early, but you never know.'

Alison thought of this man's big brown hands, working so professionally and yet so gently to free the cord from the baby's neck.

'We might have needed it anyway, if you hadn't been there for the delivery,' she said, not quite steadily.

Afterwards, when she thought about it, she knew it was just reaction that brought sudden and unexpected tears to her eyes. But knowing that didn't help the embarrassment later when she remembered Gavin's arms around her as she cried, his hands, a little awkward, drying her tears with his handkerchief.

'It's all over, and everything's fine,' he murmured.

'I'm sorry,' Alison tried to say, through her tears.

He patted her shoulder.

'There's an old Scottish saying, Have a good greet, and you'll feel better,' he told her.

'I heard the same in Edinburgh,' Alison managed to reply, and gave a watery smile.

'And do you feel better?' the doctor asked, a little cautiously, after a little while.

Alison nodded.

'I'm sorry,' she said again, awkwardly.

He looked down at her, his eyes very dark, and she thought of his arms, just a moment ago, holding her and comforting her. And then, without warning, there was the memory of the night before, when she had been unable to do anything but respond to his kiss, to the demand of his lips on hers.

She felt a slow, warm tide of colour in her cheeks. 'We'd better get back to the hospital,' she said, and turned away.

'Wait, Alison,' he said, and his hand on her arm stopped her.

If he says anything about last night, she thought, I'll — I'll die, right here on the spot.

Some of the heat had left the sun, but it was still very warm, as they stood there.

'I wanted to ask you what you thought, now that you've met Tessa,' he said abruptly.

Alison thought of the slim blonde girl, with such an air of fragility about her. She thought, too, of that surprising and unaccountable feeling of pity she had had when she realised how nervous Tessa Cameron was at meeting her. But that was a feeling she didn't want to let herself remember.

'What I thought? You mean about your sister and — Steve?' she said carefully. 'She's very pretty, and very different from — anyone else Steve has ever known. I can understand that he would find her attractive.'

There was no warmth now in the dark eyes looking down at her.

'You're not going to tell me that you don't think they really love each other?' he asked, and his voice was cool now.

Unbidden, then, there was the memory of Steve's arms around Tessa, as they'd danced to the slow music last night.

Alison shrugged.

'As I said, obviously Steve finds her attractive. But —'

It would have been wiser, she thought later, to have left it at that.

'But what?' Gavin asked.

'But that can happen without there being anything lasting about it,' she said. There was something about the stillness of his lean brown face that frightened her a little, but now that she had gone this far she might as well go on. She laughed lightly. 'I keep thinking about an old song my mother used to like — "Bewitched, Bothered and Bewildered". I — I think that's what's happened to Steve. He doesn't quite know what's hit him.'

For a long time Gavin was silent. So long that Alison had to break the silence.

'And besides,' she said, levelly now, 'I really can't see your sister coping with living on a sheep station miles from anywhere!'

'You know nothing about what my sister is capable of,' Gavin returned, scorn in his voice.

Without another word, he swung round and got into the driver's seat of the Land Rover. Alison, equally silently, climbed into the passenger seat.

It was only when they stopped in the hospital grounds that he spoke again.

'And just what do you intend doing about your feeling that Steve is making a mistake?' he asked.

'I should think Steve will see that for himself, sooner or later,' Alison returned.

His voice was low. 'If you ever do anything to hurt Tessa,' he said, not quite steadily, 'you'll have me to answer to.'

He strode ahead of her into the hospital, taking the incubator, and leaving the rest to her. And a slow, bewildering desolation engulfed Alison as she remembered sitting across the table from him in her mother's kitchen such a short time ago, laughing at something he had said.

A desolation not helped by the realisation that Tessa Cameron had two men to look out for her, to protect her. Steve Winter, and her brother.

And I'm on my own, Alison thought. And then, as she followed the doctor across to the hospital, a reviving anger took over. So what? she thought, inelegantly and defiantly. It doesn't matter to me, Gavin Cameron, I can look after myself!

And it certainly didn't seem to matter to Gavin Cameron whether they were friends or enemies, she found herself thinking in the next few days.

He was unfailingly professional and polite, when he came to do his ward rounds, when they did a late-night delivery together. But no more and no less than that.

Sometimes Alison would find Molly Barton's eyes on her, a little questioning, but the young nurse didn't say anything. She did, though, talk to Alison about the pilot, Rick Garrett. Alison had forgotten that Rick was married to Molly's sister Beth.

'I worry about them,' Molly said one day when they were having a mug of tea in the duty-room. 'I reckon running a hotel isn't the best kind of job for Rick — too many chances for him to be too sociable. And then he leaves all the work of the hotel to Beth.'

Alison had known Molly's sister Beth at school, although Beth was a few years older than her.

'They've got two kids, haven't they?' she asked. 'Didn't Beth go to Charleville to have the younger one?'

Molly nodded.

'She had kidney trouble,' she said. 'Pretty bad, she was. That kind of got Rick into line for a bit, but — well, I hear things sometimes.' She put her mug down on the table. 'I shouldn't really talk like this,' she said. 'But I kind of need to get it off my chest. I was round seeing Beth yesterday, and she really didn't look well, and there was Rick, standing rounds of drinks he can't really afford, and telling his stories!'

'I'm sorry, Molly,' Alison said, concerned. 'I wish there were something I could do to help.'

The younger girl managed to smile.

'It's not your problem, Alison,' she said. 'But — look, maybe some afternoon when you're off duty you could look in and see Beth — she'd appreciate that. And tell me if you think I'm worrying too much about her.'

Alison promised she would do that, and then it was time to go back through to the ward. They were quiet in the maternity section, and so when Brian phoned to say he was bringing Meg and baby Ruth through a few days later she was able to leave Molly in charge and go out to meet them.

'I can't believe how she's grown in a couple of weeks,' she said, looking at the baby fast asleep in her carrycot.

'What I can't believe,' Meg said, lifting out the bag with all the baby necessities in it, 'is that there was ever a life before this! Did I think I was busy, that I had too much to do? Now just about the only time I sit down is when I'm feeding her —— Oh, hi, Gavin. We're here.'

Alison hadn't heard the doctor coming. He smiled now at Brian and Meg, and nodded to her.

'We'll do her check-up over in your ward, Sister,' he said.

Baby Ruth had regained her birthweight, and Alison filled in a clinic card for her, and listened while Gavin discussed her feeding.

'Right now, Meg,' he said firmly, 'the baby is your first priority. Yes, even before you at the moment, Brian! Sounds to me as if you're trying to get back into all you used to do too quickly.'

'Too right she is, Gavin,' Brian said. 'See what I told you, Meg? Maybe you'll listen to the doctor!'

Meg smiled and nodded.

'Maybe I will,' she agreed.

Alison completed the card for the baby, and filed it. The baby decided then that all this weighing and measuring was all very well, but something more would be appreciated, so Meg sat down in the duty-room to feed her.

'I'm off to pick up this list of stores Mum needs — I'll come back for you,' Brian said.

He and Gavin went out together, and Alison made tea for Meg to have while she was feeding the baby.

'How've you been, Alison?' Meg asked softly, looking up.

The real and warm concern in her sister-in-law's eyes touched Alison more than she would have thought possible.

'I'm all right,' she said, not too steadily. And then, because Meg's concern deserved more than that, 'Look, Meg, I'm not exactly jumping for joy at the way things are, but at the same time I'm not prepared to go around with my face tripping me!'

There was relief in Meg's laughter.

'No,' she agreed, 'I wouldn't have thought you'd do that.' She hesitated. 'They're not actually engaged, are they?' she asked. 'Steve and Tessa?'

'Not as far as I know,' Alison said. She shrugged. 'But I suppose everyone is expecting that to happen pretty soon.'

Meg's hazel eyes held hers.

'And when it does?' she asked. 'Will that make it easier or harder for you?'

Alison walked over to the window and looked out, not really seeing the dusty, bleak hospital grounds.

'I don't know,' she admitted. And then, without turning round, she said, her voice low, 'Maybe I'm being foolish, but somehow I keep feeling Steve will see that she's not the right kind of girl for him. She's not an outback girl, Meg.'

It was, she thought later, Meg's silence that made her turn round.

Gavin stood in the doorway. His dark eyes studied her, and the cool hostility in them dismayed her. He had obviously heard what she had said.

Alison lifted her chin. I will not apologise, she thought fiercely. I have every right to say what I want to Meg!

But after a moment the doctor turned to Meg.

'I found the name of that herbal tea for nursing mothers,' he said. 'I've written it down for you.' He looked down at the baby in Meg's arms, drowsy and content, and his face softened. 'Have a good journey back,' he added. 'And bring Ruth to the clinic in a fortnight.'

At the door, he turned to Alison.

'Can I see you in my office, Sister Parr?' he said formally. 'As soon as you're free.'

Alison's heart sank.

'Certainly, Dr Cameron,' she replied, and she hoped her voice was as cool and as formal as his had been.

CHAPTER FOUR

'ARE you in trouble, Alison?' Meg asked anxiously.

Alison shrugged.

'If I am, I'll survive,' she said, with considerably more lightness than she felt. All right, she'd said as much to Gavin herself, but for him to hear her saying it to someone else, and in the hospital—— With some relief she saw, from the window, her brother's Land Rover draw up. 'Here's Brian. Let me carry the baby out—I want every possible contact with my niece!'

When she had said goodbye to Brian and Meg, and promised she'd be out at the station as soon as possible, Alison took a deep breath and headed for Gavin's office.

To her dismay, Matron was there too. Alison couldn't resist glaring at the doctor, hoping her frosty look said what she dared not put into words—that there was no need to involve Matron in this, for surely it was something private that concerned only the two of them.

But Matron's first words disarmed her completely.

'I've been put out of my office,' she said cheerfully. 'The electricians are in. That's why we're meeting in here. I meant to have a word with you yesterday, but I got tied up.'

For a moment, Gavin's eyes met Alison's. He knew, she thought, still angry. He knew I'd think it was because of what he heard me say to Meg. He might have told me it was purely a hospital thing.

'Well, now,' Matron said briskly, 'you know, of course, that Sister Butler is back. But she's decided that

she doesn't feel she can work full-time now, so she's
going to continue doing theatre — as far as possible,
she'll be on call for any theatre emergencies too. But
she was also the sister who accompanied the doctor on
any emergency calls to any of the outlying stations, and
she isn't going to be available for that.'

Matron smiled at Alison, encouragingly and posi-
tively, and Alison's heart sank, for she could see very
clearly where this was leading.

'It looks from the bookings as if you have a fairly
quiet time ahead in Maternity, Sister Parr. In any case,
I'd do it myself, if necessary.'

Matron looked at Alison expectantly.

And after a moment, looking straight ahead, determined she would not meet Gavin's eyes, Alison said,
very stiffly, very correctly, that of course she would be
prepared to go with the doctor, if it was necessary.

Maybe it won't happen, she told herself over the next
few days, as she and Molly looked after their three
patients, and the three new babies. The three deliveries
had been very straightforward, but one of the young
mothers gave them a fright the day after her baby was
born, when Alison, coming over late at night to check
her ward, which she occasionally did, heard the shallow
and irregular breathing before she reached the bed. She
sent the night nurse to the office to phone for the
doctor, but she knew, as she worked swiftly, that she
couldn't wait for him to get there.

'Tell him postpartum haemorrhage, rapid pulse, and
falling blood-pressure,' she said to the frightened young
nurse.

She elevated the foot of the bed, and as she did so her
training and experience took over, so that she was able
to work swiftly and efficiently, because she didn't know
how long it would take the doctor to get there.

Ergometrine intravenously would act immediately, but she would waste valuable time if she was unable to inject the vein, and already the young woman on the bed was in a collapsed state.

She was conscious of the young nurse returning, but her whole attention was on the steadiness of her own hands. Careful, she told herself. That was it, the needle had found the vein, and almost immediately she could see the reaction. By the time Gavin hurried in, the young woman's condition was beginning to stabilise, but Alison had decided to set up an oxytocin drip.

Without a word, the doctor got to work with her, adjusting the drip, checking the blood-pressure, standing by while Alison changed the pads she had used.

'She'll do,' he said at last. 'But I'll hang around in my office for a bit, just in case.'

As they walked across to the main building, he looked at her.

'You're not on night duty,' he said, a little abruptly. 'What made you come over?'

In the darkness, Alison felt herself colour.

'I don't know,' she said, knowing she sounded defensive. 'Sometimes I just have a feeling I should check. Look, Nurse Barton would have gone around in half an hour, and she would have seen, but —'

'But it's a very good thing for this patient that you did have that feeling,' Gavin said soberly. 'Don't ever discount feelings like that—they go beyond training, experience, whatever.'

They had reached the main building, and he looked down at her. She could see, in the dim light of the doorway, that he needed to shave. There was a disturbing intimacy about this realisation that made her say goodnight very abruptly and go on round the corner to the nurses' home.

But after that drama life on the maternity ward was quiet, with Gavin coming in to do his rounds, visiting time in the afternoon and the evening, and the three babies and mothers all making steady progress.

And then, just when Alison was beginning to feel less anxious about having to accompany the doctor on any emergency calls, he came into the ward early one afternoon.

'Sister Parr—sorry, but I need you to come with me. There's a stockman been gored at Borramunga. Rick Garrett's away in Charleville, so the plane isn't available. We'll have to drive—how soon can you be ready?'

Alison looked at her ward, and then at Molly's eyes, wide and anxious.

'Five minutes,' she said firmly.

And when he had gone, his white coat flying behind him, she turned to the young nurse.

'It's all right, Molly, you'll cope. Matron is there if you need her—and I should be back either late tonight, or at least tomorrow.'

'What if another patient has a haemorrhage?' Molly asked shakily. 'Or—or something happens to one of the babies?'

Alison put her hand on the girl's arm.

'You're a fully trained nurse, Molly,' she reminded the girl. 'If anything does happen, you'll know what to do.'

But she took a moment, before hurrying to the waiting Land Rover, to look in to Matron's office and point out that Molly Barton would appreciate some back-up.

Gavin had already started the engine, and as soon as Alison had climbed in he got going. Neither of them said anything until they were clear of the small town, and heading out into the scrubland.

Borramunga—Steve's station—wasn't as far out as Blue Rock Ridge, and, as Alison knew very well, the journey would take less than two hours. But still her heart sank at the thought of that time sitting in the confines of the Land Rover with Gavin Cameron.

'I've asked Beth Garrett to try to get a message to Rick,' the doctor said, when the dusty small town was behind them. 'We may find this man can't be brought back with us, and I'd like to know the plane is on standby.'

There was a stretcher at the back of the Land Rover, along with the rest of the medical equipment kept there.

'How bad does it sound?' Alison asked, grateful to remain completely professional.

'Seems as if he's been pretty badly gored,' Gavin said. 'They haven't risked moving him—it doesn't happen too often, but often enough for everyone to know the risks of internal injuries. So a bumpy ride back in the Land Rover could be out of the question, but we'll only know that when we see him.'

A little further on, he talked about the drama the other night.

'But you didn't really need me,' he said. 'You'd done all the right things, and she was through the worst.'

It's an olive-branch, this, and I should accept it, Alison told herself.

'I was still mighty glad to know you were there,' she told him truthfully.

'I'm sure you know your Maggie Myles inside out,' the doctor said then, without taking his eyes off the road ahead. 'Postpartum haemorrhage is one of the most serious complications in obstetrics. That young woman's life was in your hands, Alison. Your good management kept the blood loss under control.'

'I certainly knew how serious it could be,' Alison agreed. 'And yes, of course Maggie Myles is any midwife's bible. What really worried me, though — afterwards, when I had time to think about it — was that there wasn't any reason for it happening. She's not a multipara, this is her first baby, and there was no placenta adherence.'

'I know,' he agreed. 'And because of that I want her to have a complete gynaecological check-up. One possible reason is fibroid tumours, and I want that checked out.'

There was silence then, for a while, as he negotiated the ruts on the track.

I should do my bit in the conversation line, Alison thought.

'We have one river crossing,' she said. 'Should be all right, because we've had no rain, but it can be pretty crook in the wet. Trouble now is we could bog down in the sand.'

Gavin glanced at her for a moment, and smiled.

'It's all right, I know how to deal with that,' he told her. 'Deflate the tyres, and find some brushwood, that should give us enough of a grip.'

'You're learning about the outback right enough,' Alison said.

Again he glanced at her, before giving his full attention to the track.

'The outback isn't new to me,' he said. 'My grandparents had a station near Longreach, and I used to spend holidays there as a boy, before they retired to join us in Canberra.' He paused, then said, a little awkwardly, 'I've always had a hankering to come back. That's why I took this chance now.'

For some reason, this surprised Alison.

'You liked the outback enough to come back to it?' she asked.

'So did you,' he returned, without looking at her.

But they both knew this was dangerous ground, her coming back, and he went on quickly.

'My grandfather used to say, after they came to Canberra, that it was a good life, and he felt they'd earned it, but there were times when he longed for — he called it the profound silence of the outback. He missed the vastness, he missed these distant mountains. And — well, I'd only known all this as a boy, but I could understand what he was saying. In a way, I came back for him as well as for me.'

'Is he still alive, your grandfather?' Alison asked, after a moment.

Gavin shook his head.

'He died fifteen years ago, and my grandmother soon after that.' And then, his voice carefully level, he said, 'My parents died a year ago, in a car crash. That's one of the reasons I felt it would be a good idea to make a complete break, go somewhere else.' Again he paused. 'For me and for Tessa.'

Alison thought of her own parents, of the strength and the warm security of her family. Even in the time she had been away, it had helped her, knowing they were there, knowing she would go back to them. It was a devastating thought to ask herself how she would feel if they weren't there, if she had to live the rest of her life without them.

'I didn't know that, Gavin,' she said, her voice low.

'No, you wouldn't,' he replied.

Alison knew, then and afterwards, that he had given her the opening and the opportunity to ask more about Tessa, to talk about her coming here, and meeting

Steve, but she didn't take it. Instead, she asked him about Canberra.

'I've never been there myself,' she said. 'But Brian and Meg went there for their honeymoon, and Meg thought it was terrific.'

'When were they there?' Gavin asked. 'What time of year, I mean?'

'Autumn,' Alison told him. 'Meg sent me a postcard, to Edinburgh, of the trees around the lake, all red and gold. But she said the thing that struck her most, coming from the outback, was how green all the back yards were.'

'I hope you didn't say that to any of your Edinburgh friends,' Gavin commented. 'You and I know that a back yard is a garden — I doubt if folks in Edinburgh would realise that!'

They had crossed the river by then, and soon the homestead of Borramunga was in sight. It was more than two years since Alison had been here. She could remember how she had felt that day. Excited about going away, about the places she would see, the work she would do. A little sad, yes, but underneath the sadness, underneath the excitement, there had been the certainty, deep and steady, that she would be coming back here. Back to Steve, back to Borramunga.

And now, she thought, I am back at Borramunga. But not coming to it as my home, as Steve's wife.

'I'm sorry about this, Alison,' Gavin said unexpectedly, as he turned off the engine.

She knew very well what he meant, but she pretended not to understand, because she didn't want him to say any more.

'Taking me away from the hospital?' she queried. 'It's good for Molly to cope on her own.'

For a moment, taking her completely by surprise, his hand covered hers.

'I mean about coming here. I wish, for you, it had been anywhere but Borramunga.' There was warmth and concern in his voice.

And Alison thought, with complete clarity, Gavin Cameron being unpleasant I can take. But Gavin Cameron being nice, being kind and thoughtful, I don't think I can!

'It's all right,' she said, more brusquely than she meant to, and she turned away from him and swung herself down from the Land Rover.

Steve came hurrying over to them, his face anxious.

'He's pretty bad, Gavin,' he said, after a hurried greeting—and his anxiety about his stockman, Alison thought, prevented him from any awkwardness about seeing her. 'We didn't move him—he's in the yard. We covered him up, he was shivering, although it's mighty hot.'

The two men strode round the side of the house, Alison hurrying to keep up with them. There were a few men round the form on the ground, and a woman.

'Bluey's wife,' Steve said briefly, as the woman moved aside, and Gavin knelt by the injured stockman, examining him swiftly, expertly.

'Send someone for the stretcher from the Land Rover, and we'll take him into the house,' he said. His eyes met Alison's. 'We'll clean him up, give him something for the pain, put a dressing on, and start fighting infection. But I need him in hospital.'

She knew, because she had seen the momentary hesitation of his hands, that he was afraid of renal damage. And that could only be assessed in hospital.

Gavin himself, with Alison helping, eased the unconscious man on to the stretcher. Two of the other stockmen carried him into the house, to a small bed-room off the kitchen.

Gavin turned to the man's wife.

'We need to have Bluey in hospital,' he said quietly. 'And that track's mighty bumpy. I'm going to have Rick Garrett come in and take him back. Can you come with him?'

The woman was white now, but controlled.

'Sure I can, Doc,' she said steadily. 'I'll pick up a couple of things in the house, and then I'll stay here with Bluey.'

For a moment, her workworn hand gently touched the unconscious man's cheek.

'Is there anything I can do for him?' she asked. 'To make him more comfortable, like?'

Gavin shook his head.

'He's going to be out for quite a while,' he told her. 'Long enough for the plane to get him to the hospital. You go off now, and get whatever you need — Sister Parr and I will be heading back as soon as possible. I want to be there when you and Bluey arrive.'

She had just gone when Steve came through, carrying two mugs of tea, and thick sandwiches.

'You heading back right away, Gavin?' he asked. 'I thought you'd need something to eat, the two of you. A radio call just came through from the hospital — they've got hold of Rick Garrett, he's on his way back to Namboola Creek, he should be here for Bluey in two hours. I've told the men to get the lights ready at the landing-strip.'

Gavin looked at his watch.

'Which means we need to move,' he said. 'Steve, call them back and ask Dr Mac to be on standby, in case. Drink your tea, Alison — we can eat as we go.'

They left Steve with the injured man, to stay until his wife got back, and went back out to the Land Rover.

'You think kidney damage?' Alison asked, as they drove away from the homestead.

Gavin nodded. 'Possibly spleen too,' he said. 'I'm not happy about that. We need to have him in, and we may need to send him on to Charleville, depending on what I find.'

They were both quiet then, eating the sandwiches Steve had given them. The station cook had poured the rest of the tea into a flask, and when they had finished eating Alison managed, in spite of the bumpy track, to pour them each half a mug of tea.

It was already dark when they crossed the river, but the Land Rover had strong and powerful lights. So Alison was surprised when Gavin drew up, and switched off the engine.

'I'm sorry,' he said. 'I'm bushed, Alison — I was up most of last night with a patient's ulcer. I'm not prepared to risk driving on a track like this unless I close my eyes for a bit. Give me half an hour, then wake me.'

He leaned back, and even in the dim light Alison could see that he was exhausted.

'Don't be ridiculous,' she said, concern making her voice sharp. 'We don't have to stop.'

The doctor shook his head.

'Sorry,' he said, his voice blurred. 'I just need to close my eyes, half an hour will do, then I'll be fine. But I can't drive like this — I could have us off the track.'

Alison gave him a little push.

'You can't, but I can,' she said. 'Move over.'

Gavin opened his eyes.

'It's too heavy for you,' he told her.

'I've been driving one of these since I was sixteen,' Alison said shortly. 'Move, Gavin.'

He stayed awake long enough, she was sure, to see that she could indeed drive the heavy Land Rover. Then he fell asleep, first leaning against the window beside him, and then slowly keeling over on Alison's shoulder.

She drove on through the dusk, and then the darkness, steadily, competently — but was very conscious, all the time, of the weight of Gavin's dark head against her, of the intimacy of this man she disliked so much, asleep here so close to her.

The lights of Namboola Creek were just visible in the distance when she had to stop, because the arm Gavin was leaning on had gone to sleep. She drew the Land Rover to the side of the road, and carefully tried to ease her numb arm out.

Gavin opened his eyes.

'Alison?' he said hazily.

There was just enough moonlight for her to think that somehow he looked younger, still half asleep.

She explained about her arm being numb, that she'd had to stop.

'But we're almost there,' she said. 'Half an hour, and we'll make it. We should certainly be there before the plane gets back.'

He was sitting up now, and her shoulder felt strangely cold without his warm weight on it. And there was something in his stillness beside her in the cab that made her uncomfortable all at once.

'Do you want to drive now?' she asked him.

'Sure,' he said. 'Give my your arm.'

He rubbed her arm, gently and firmly, bringing life back to it. Then his fingers were still, encircling her arm.

'Thanks, I'm fine now,' Alison said quickly.

He didn't move.

In some strange way, it seemed to Alison that the world had narrowed to the two of them, herself and the doctor, so near to each other that it needed only one small movement to ——

She moved back, away from him.

'Let's change over,' she said, and opened the door and went round the front of the Land Rover.

As she reached the passenger door, Gavin jumped down. Alison moved back, but not quickly enough. His arms encircled her, holding her very close to him, stopping her from getting away — if she had tried to, or wanted to.

'I refuse to kiss you again in the cab of a confounded Land Rover!' he said, and there was warm, sleepy laughter in his voice. 'It cramps my style!'

CHAPTER FIVE

GAVIN's lips were warm and demanding on hers. And for Alison there was no thought of resisting, no possibility of anything but her body's immediate response to his.

Immediate, and somehow treacherous, she thought dazedly, when they drew apart at last.

'And that, too, was because I wanted to,' Gavin said, not quite steadily.

What had happened, Alison wondered, to all the hostility and coolness between them? On his side, and on hers. For she knew very well that all she wanted right now was to go back into his arms, to feel his lips on hers again.

She turned away from him, confused.

'What is it, Alison?' he asked, and the gentleness of his voice unnerved her completely.

'I shouldn't——' She stopped, not knowing what it was she wanted to say, not sure what it was she felt.

He put one hand under her chin and turned her head round, so that she had to look at him.

'You shouldn't have enjoyed that as much as you did, when you're supposed to be heartbroken about Steve Winter?' he asked her.

She felt her cheeks grow warm, for he had put into words exactly her confused and troubled feelings.

'Not to mention,' Gavin went on, and now there was warm amusement in his voice, 'the fact that you dislike me heartily?'

'I wasn't under the impression that I was just your

favourite person either,' Alison returned, managing, with an effort, to recover a little.

'There's another saying from Yorkshire,' he said. 'There's nowt so queer as folk. Maybe that's as good an explanation as we'll find, Alison, for this — very strange reaction you and I have to each other.'

He was laughing at her again, and she knew she should have felt angry. But her whole body was still warm and — langorous, she thought, was the word she wanted, and it was difficult to feel angry. Difficult to feel anything but this disturbing way she did feel.

'We should be getting back,' she said. 'You want to be at the hospital when the plane gets back.'

'We would have seen the lights of the plane, and we would have heard it,' Gavin assured her. 'At least, I think we would have. But you're right, we should get back.'

But as she turned away he caught her hand and swung her back.

'If I'd been Steve Winter, I'd never have let you go away,' he said, his voice low.

Alison lifted her chin.

'No one tells me what to do!' she said.

The doctor laughed softly.

'That I can believe. All right, maybe I wouldn't have tried telling you what to do, but I'd have made damned sure you didn't want to go!'

He was very close to her, so close that she wasn't sure whether it was his heart thudding unevenly, or her own. And for this moment, she knew, with disturbing certainty, that she didn't care who he was, or what she really thought of him. She wanted to feel his arms around her, his lips warm and demanding on hers, his lean body hard against hers.

And then he moved back.

'This isn't the time or the place,' he murmured.

It sounded like a promise, Alison thought, trying to regain control of herself.

'Just one thing, though. Surely there's no need for you and me to go on feeling so hostile to each other?' he said. 'We work together — inevitably, here in Namboola Creek, we have a lot of contact. I understand how you feel about Steve and my sister, and you understand how I feel. Can't we leave it at that, and declare a truce?' He held out his hand.

Alison hesitated for a moment, and then held out her own, determined to behave as if that bewildering longing to return to his arms had never engulfed her.

They were back at the hospital an hour before the pilot of the small plane, accompanied by one of the young nurses from the general ward, arrived with the injured stockman and his wife.

It was late, and it seemed unnecessary to have Jean Butler called from home, so Alison scrubbed up and assisted Gavin in Theatre. His examination confirmed what he had suspected — that there was damage to the spleen as well as to the kidneys.

She watched as he palpated the spleen gently, and saw that even though Bluey was unconscious he winced when the doctor's hand was withdrawn.

'Referred rebound tenderness, and definitely enlarged,' Gavin murmured. 'I'm going to send him through to Charleville — this damage needs to be assessed by scanning. We'll have the Flying Doctor service; I want to be sure he'll have medical attention on the way.'

Alison stayed in the theatre, cleaning up, while he went to tell the stockman's wife what was happening, and to radio a call for a plane from the Flying Doctor service to be sent to take both of them to Charleville. When he came back, Alison had made a pot of tea.

'If you can help me to get him out to the Land Rover,' Gavin said, 'I'll go up to the airstrip — I don't want to keep these fellows waiting; the plane's leaving right away. Tea — just what we all need.'

Bluey's wife put her empty cup down and said carefully, 'He's going to be all right, isn't he?'

For a moment, Gavin's eyes met Alison's.

'He should be,' he said then, just as carefully. 'He does need more specialised assessment than we can do here; that's why I'm sending him to Charleville. Look, he isn't just going to get up and be his old self in a few days; don't expect that. But, barring anything unforeseen, yes, he should be all right.'

Alison watched the big Land Rover, which was used as an ambulance, heading off through the silent town, towards the airstrip, and she was glad that Gavin had been honest with the stockman's wife.

Then she went into her room in the nurses' home, to go to bed. It had been a long day, she thought, and a very strange one.

She took off her uniform, had a quick bath, and then, in her blue cotton shortie nightie, sat down at the mirror to brush her hair. And with the brush in her hand she paused, and touched her lips. The girl in the mirror looked back at her steadily, her grey eyes wide, remembering how she had felt in Gavin Cameron's arms.

And remembering, too, how they had parted, with an agreement that there would be a truce between them.

But she didn't deceive herself about that. She knew very well that the doctor had meant what he said when he told her that if she ever did anything to hurt his sister she would have him to answer to.

And as she sat there, staring into the mirror, the though that had come to her before, the thought that he had laughed at, returned. Surely it was possible that Gavin, feeling as protective as he did towards his sister, would go to any lengths to keep anyone from coming between Steve and her? Anyone — but most of all Alison Parr. The way he had kissed her, the way he had held her — couldn't that have been done deliberately, to keep things going smoothly between Steve and Tessa?

And why, she wondered, should she find that thought so distressing and so disturbing?

A truce, he had said. So — a truce, but a guarded one, Alison reminded herself.

Not that she had any intention of setting out to come between Tessa Cameron and Steve. She was still very sure that Steve himself would come to see that this girl could never fit into life on an outback sheep and cattle station.

And after that, when Steve had realised and admitted this?

That thought opened the door to too many questions. If he turned back to Alison, then would Gavin blame her for the break-up? Would her pride let her accept Steve back again? Would Gavin — and his sister — stay on here in Namboola Creek if Tessa and Steve parted? How would she herself feel if that happened?

At that stage, Alison told herself firmly that she was being ridiculous. There was nothing she could do about any one of these imponderables, nothing but wait and see. See what happened, see how she felt.

She knew very well what her mother would say: You're crossing far too many bridges you might never come to, my girl.

In a determined effort to turn her thoughts in other directions, she set off, on her next afternoon off, to visit Molly's sister Beth at the hotel.

It was hot, as she walked along the dusty street, under the shade of the mulga trees, and there was a heaviness in the air, a leaden feel, that made her hope the rains might come soon. Her mother had said on the phone the other night how badly they needed rain, and she had seen on the journey to Borramunga, how desperately dry the land was.

'Hello, Alison.'

Deep in her thoughts, she hadn't seen the girl coming towards her. It was Tessa Cameron. Her long fair hair was tied back from her face, and she wore a cotton dress that was the same blue as her eyes. She looked very pretty, Alison thought. She also looked extremely apprehensive.

'Hello, Tessa,' she said, stopping, her voice carefully polite. 'I'm sorry, I was so busy thinking about how much we need rain, I didn't see you.'

'Yes, everything's very dry,' Tessa agreed, equally polite. She looked at Alison, and Alison looked back. Neither of them, Alison thought, knew what to say or what to do next. 'I believe Bluey's on the mend now.'

'Yes, he's being sent back to us here in a few days,' Alison said.

Once again the two girls looked at each other.

And then, as if she had made up her mind, Tessa said quickly, nervously, 'I've been wanting to get the chance to speak to you, Alison. It—it's a bit foolish for us to pretend that—that——' She stopped.

'To pretend that Steve didn't decide he preferred you to me?' Alison asked steadily.

Tessa flushed. 'I just think maybe we could talk,' she

said, her voice low. 'Maybe if we did you might understand——'

'Understand what?' Alison asked.

The younger girl lifted her chin.

'That Steve and I love each other,' she said, and now her voice was steady too. 'That he didn't want to hurt you, but it's happened.' And when Alison, somehow at a loss with this direct confrontation, didn't reply, Tessa went on, 'Maybe it's you and Steve who should be talking—I don't know. I just think some talking needs to be done!'

Oh, no, Alison thought, with certainty. The last thing I need in my life right now is to have this girl telling me how much she and Steve love each other. Or to have Steve himself tell me! No way!

'I'm sorry,' she said. 'I really don't think anything could be achieved by that.'

'Couldn't we at least go and have a cup of tea together?' Tessa asked.

Alison shook her head, and explained that she was on her way to visit Beth Garrett. She said goodbye then, but as she turned in the door of the hotel she looked back. Tessa was walking on down the street, and her head was held high.

And I suppose, Alison thought, she'll tell Big Brother that she tried to be friends, and I refused. But in spite of the defiance of her thoughts she knew very well that she needn't have gone to visit Molly's sister that day; Molly would have understood if she'd left it for another time.

These last few days, since she and the doctor had declared their truce, she had found the change between them at work made things so different. Gavin was always completely professional on the ward, but sometimes now he would have a quick cup of tea with Molly and Alison in the duty-room, and then he would relax, put his feet up on the desk, and ask Alison about Edinburgh, or he would tell them about his time in the Flying Doctor service.

It would be a great pity if that were to change, if he were to revert to the old cool distance, Alison thought, but there was nothing else she could have done.

She went on into the hotel.

Beth Garrett came through from the pub, a glass and a drying-cloth in her hand.

'Alison, how nice to see you,' she said, obviously surprised. 'I knew it was too early for the kids to be back from school, and I wondered who it was. Come on through to the kitchen and I'll make tea.'

Alison followed her through to the kitchen, and she thought Molly was right; Beth did look tired, and there were dark shadows under her eyes.

'Molly talks so much about you,' Beth said, as she sat down at the scrubbed kitchen table beside Alison. 'She's really enjoying working with you.' She hesitated, but only for a moment. 'I'm sorry things didn't work out for you and Steve, Alison.'

I'm sorry too, Alison thought, and once again she could feel the shock and the bleakness she had felt when Steve told her.

'Just one of those things,' she shrugged, with considerably more lightness than she felt. How are things with you, Beth? I've seen Rick a couple of times — he never seems to mind dropping everything and flying for us.'

'Oh, no, he loves it,' Beth agreed. She smiled. 'Gives a bit of excitement to life for him. Things can be pretty quiet at this time of year in the hotel.'

'Busy enough to keep you working pretty hard, I should think,' Alison said.

Beth shrugged. 'I don't mind,' she said. She asked Alison about her folks, about Brian's and Meg's baby, and they talked about people they had both known at school. And then, when Alison rose to go, she said impulsively, 'Are you all right, Beth? You look tired.'

Beth had been standing up too, but she sat down.

'I'm pregnant again,' she said flatly. 'I haven't told anyone, not Rick, not my folks, not Molly. I was fine with Simon on the way, but with Brenda I had kidney trouble real bad, and Dr Mac said I shouldn't think of having any more. So—so when I found out I just kept quiet.'

Alison sat down too. Without a word, she reached for the big brown teapot and poured more tea for both of them.

'How far are you?' she asked, and Beth said she was about halfway.

'And how do you feel?' Alison went on, keeping her voice brisk and practical.

'Not too good sometimes,' Beth admitted. She managed to smile, a little shakily. 'I'm real glad I told you, Alison, somehow.'

Before she left, Alison made Beth promise she would tell Rick, tell her folks, and tell Molly. And, most of all, see the doctor.

'You've got to have this pregnancy carefully supervised, Beth,' she said.

Beth nodded. 'I knew that,' she admitted. 'I'll be along to see Dr Cameron tomorrow. Maybe this baby wasn't planned, Alison, but I want it very much.'

Gavin, a few days later, mentioned to Alison that Beth had been to see him, and that he would be keeping a very careful check on her condition from now on.

'I've had a look at her file,' he said quietly. 'We'll be mighty lucky if she gets away with this pregnancy without real problems. Any possibility of renal failure, and we'll have to act. But if we can get her to seven months, the baby will have a chance. Thanks for persuading her to come and see me.'

There had been no change in his manner towards her since the day she met Tessa, and Alison, with somewhat unwilling gratitude, realised that Tessa hadn't said anything to her brother. Because if she had there was no way Gavin would have accepted Alison's mother's invitation to come out with Alison and spend the weekend at Blue Rock Ridge.

'I've made excuses a couple of times before, when your mother has asked me,' Gavin said when he told her. 'I felt this time I had to say yes. And besides, I wanted to. Do you mind?'

'No, I don't mind,' Alison replied, more than a little taken aback to realise just how true this was.

They left early in the morning, in Gavin's Land Rover, while it was still fresh and cool. For a little while they talked about the hospital, and Gavin told her that old Dr Mac was only too pleased to be back in harness for a couple of days. The stockman from Borramunga would be brought back to them soon, before he was allowed to go back to the station.

And then, as if by common consent, they were both quiet.

From the riverbed, Alison always loved the view of the distant mountains, blue and hazy in the early morning light. The vastness of the plain, the clear canopy of the summer sky — this was what she had missed, what she had longed for, while she was away.

'I'd love to reach those mountains,' Gavin said, almost to himself.

'We could ride there,' Alison told him. 'If we leave early tomorrow morning we could be back by sundown.

We could picnic at Blue Rock — you can't see it properly from here, it rises at the end of the ridge. There's a cave, and there's a couple of tunnels — Brian and I used to go there when we were kids. I haven't been for years. The wind whistles in the cave — it's kind of eerie.'

Just over the river, they stopped and had coffee from the flask Alison had brought, and sandwiches.

'Although we don't really need them,' Alison said. 'Mum will have an enormous breakfast ready for us.'

There was a breeze blowing here beside the river, and Alison's hair blew across her face. Gently Gavin pushed it back. For a moment his fingers lingered on the curve of her cheek. His eyes were very dark as he looked down at her.

'You look younger here — more carefree,' he said softly.

'So do you,' Alison returned, and it was true. Here, in an open-necked shirt and jeans, his thick dark hair blown too by the wind, the big doctor did look younger.

'Come on,' he said, and took her hand. 'We'd better not keep your mother and that breakfast waiting. We have plenty of time.'

He stood up and pulled her to her feet. And then he kept her hand in his as they walked back to the Land Rover.

'Plenty of time for what?' Alison asked, very casually.

'All sorts of things,' he said, equally casually.

What is it about this man, Alison thought, half annoyed, half amused, that makes me take much more out of what he's just said than I would with any other man?

The homestead was in sight now. And Alison found herself wishing, foolishly, just for a moment, that she and Gavin were coming here for this visit with no shadows between them, no complications.

CHAPTER SIX

IT WAS strange, Alison thought afterwards, strange and disturbing, that Gavin seemed to know what she was thinking.

'This weekend,' he said, as they got back into the Land Rover, 'I refuse to think of anything but being here with you to visit your folks. I'm carrying no excess baggage, and I hope neither are you!' He smiled, and just for a moment his hand brushed hers. 'And now for that breakfast you promised your mother would have ready for us!'

The breakfast was all Alison had expected and more. There was steak, sausages, tomatoes, bacon, eggs, thick slices of toast, and a huge pot of tea.

'That was magnificent, Mary,' Gavin said when he had finished. He looked across at Alison. 'You reckon you feel strong enough to walk across and visit your niece now?'

There had been a message from Meg when they arrived that she'd just got the baby off to sleep, but she'd probably be awake by the time they had breakfast.

'I'll help with the dishes first, Mum,' Alison said, as her mother began clearing the plates away.

'No, you won't,' her mother said firmly. 'Old Jessie will do them when she comes in. Off you go, now. Dad and Brian will be back later—there's word of a horse gone wild, chasing the brood mares—they've gone off to see if they can track him down. Meg and Brian will be over tonight, of course, so we'll all eat together.'

The cottage was only five minutes' walk from the big house, and they were halfway when they heard the baby crying.

'She's awake all right,' Gavin remarked. 'And a fine healthy-sounding pair of lungs.'

Meg's short brown curls were rumpled, and she obviously hadn't had time to put even a touch of lipstick on.

'Here,' she said unceremoniously, and handed the baby to Alison. 'And if you tell me it's colic and she'll outgrow it, I don't know what I'll do!'

A little nervously, Alison held the baby up against her shoulder and patted her.

'You can hold her tighter, she won't bite,' said Meg, and now she was smiling. 'I thought you were experienced with babies, Alison!'

'Not this size,' Alison pointed out. 'Newly born, yes, and then older, but I haven't had much to do with them in between.'

The baby had stopped crying, and Alison sat down on the couch to have a good look at her. There was a definite fluff of hair now, and baby Ruth's eyes were the same clear blue as her father's.

'That's better,' Alison said softly. 'We didn't come all this way just to hear how loudly you can cry, Miss Ruth!'

The blue eyes focused on her face, and after a moment's thought the baby smiled.

'You little pet,' Alison murmured, and kissed the soft cheek. 'Meg, she's adorable!'

'I know,' her mother agreed complacently. 'But boy, does she let us know when things aren't to her liking!'

Alison looked up then, to find Gavin's eyes resting on her as she held the baby. His lean brown face was very still, and his eyes very dark, and with a warmth in them that brought a wave of colour to her cheeks.

He held out his arms for the baby and took her firmly.

'She has to let you know if things aren't right,' he said to Meg. 'Remember, she's dealing with learner parents — it's up to her to lick you into shape!'

They stayed with Meg and the baby for a little while, then Alison took Gavin over to the stables. The dogs found them there, and greeted Alison with wild delight, and Gavin with only slightly more restrained pleasure.

'If we're going riding early tomorrow, we'll have to make sure they're shut inside,' Alison said. 'It would be too much for them.'

It was an easy, pleasant day, she thought later. She and Gavin walked around the homestead and the outbuildings, and down to the river. In the searing heat of the afternoon they sat in the shade of the wide veranda. At first they talked — about Alison's time in Edinburgh, about Gavin's experiences with the Flying Doctor service, about Canberra. And then, both of them becoming drowsy, they were quiet.

Alison woke from a light doze to see that Gavin was still asleep, his dark head back on a pillow in the big comfortable cane chair. She could see now that he looked more rested, more relaxed, that he had been looking tired in the last few days, at the hospital.

He opened his eyes then, and, seeing her confusion at being found studying him, he smiled, a slow, sleepy smile that somehow made him look younger. It was a strange thing, Alison thought, bewildered, that she should find this man so disturbing. Her thoughts and her feelings about him had been so clear-cut at first. She had disliked him, she had resented his arrogance, and she had been furious at the things he had said to her.

But there was the way she had felt in his arms, and there was the way she had come to feel about him as they worked together.

'I'd like to say penny for your thoughts,' Gavin said lazily, 'but maybe they're not for sale?'

'I was wondering if you'd like a cup of tea,' Alison said quickly and completely untruthfully. And somehow she had the feeling that this man knew very well that her thoughts had certainly not been on offering him tea.

It was early evening before her father and her brother came back, reporting that they hadn't managed to find the wild horse.

'But he's been chasing the brumbies; we'll have to get out after him again,' Jim Parr said. 'Hasn't been fighting with any of them, but we don't want him starting.'

'When I was a boy,' Gavin said, 'spending holidays with my grandparents, what I wanted most in the world was to tame a brumby.'

'Alison did, when she was a kid,' Brian told him. 'Remember, Alison?'

Gavin looked across the big kitchen table at Alison.

'Was it a good feeling?' he asked her, smiling.

'It was wonderful,' Alison said, remembering the thrill of the wild young colt responding to her commands, and eventually letting her ride him.

The baby slept while they were eating, but soon after they had finished she woke, and Brian and Meg decided to go back home before Meg fed her.

'In the hope that she'll let us crash for two or three hours,' Meg said, as they left.

'And if you two are having a real early start, you shouldn't be too late getting off to bed,' Mary Parr said briskly. 'Caught you yawning just now, Gavin.'

Alison stood up.

'If you're wise,' she said, 'you don't argue with my mother.'

'I wouldn't dream of it,' Gavin assured her. And then, laughter in his eyes, 'And I'd think twice before arguing with her daughter too.'

The big, rambling old house had only one bathroom, so Alison helped her mother to tidy up in the kitchen, until Gavin called through that the bathroom was clear. His door was closed when she went along to bath, and she hesitated for a moment, a little disappointed that he hadn't waited to say goodnight to her. But he had undoubtedly been very sleepy, she reminded herself.

She lingered in her bath, half asleep herself, and when she padded barefoot back to her bedroom, her short cotton dressing-gown over her nightie, her hair was still tied up on top of her head. Just as she was going into her bedroom Gavin's door, next to hers, opened.

'I just wanted to say goodnight,' he said. 'I was beginning to think you'd fallen asleep in the bath.'

His eyes, dark and amused, took in her appearance — pink and flushed, she knew, and tendrils of hair escaping from the ribbon.

'I almost did,' she admitted.

'You look like a little girl with your hair tied up like that,' he said softly. And then, his mouth twitching a little as he suppressed a smile, 'Well, a grown-up little girl, let's say.'

Alison coloured, very conscious that her cotton nightie and dressing-gown were very skimpy. And even more conscious that all the doctor had on was boxer shorts.

'I'll call you in the morning,' she said quickly. 'Unless you want to change your mind about the long ride?'

He shook his head.

'I want to reach these mountains, and I want to see your cave,' he said. He looked down at her. 'Goodnight, Alison,' he murmured.

That was all. Not that she had expected him to kiss her, she told herself when she was lying in bed. Or wanted him to. And anyway, considering what had happened on the other occasions he had kissed her, it was probably just as well.

Like putting a match to fireworks, she thought. And then, sleepily, And what a strange thing, that; it must be a sort of chemistry, a body chemistry, that bypasses things like being friends, liking each other, and goes straight on to this ridiculous fireworks thing.

But somehow, after this day they had spent together, she realised that she couldn't honestly say that she didn't like this man. Already, in spite of the way they had started off, they had shared so much in their work. She had come to see that Gavin was a good and a caring doctor, and she knew, without deceiving herself, that he thought of her as a good nurse. And more than that, there had been, today, this easy and casual companionship between them. She had enjoyed that; there was no use pretending otherwise.

It was still dark when her alarm clock woke her, and she dressed quickly and went through to the silent kitchen. Coffee, she thought, to wake us both up, and as soon as it was ready she took a mug along to the room Gavin was sleeping in.

It had been pretty warm through the night, and he had thrown even the sheet off. He was lying on his back, and he looked strangely defenceless asleep.

'Gavin,' she said, and touched his shoulder.

Like most doctors and nurses, he was awake instantly. And just as instantly realising where he was.

'Coffee, to wake you up,' she told him. 'I'll be in the kitchen, getting our food ready.'

'Be there in five minutes,' he promised, and he was, reaching the kitchen just as she finished packing the food she and her mother had prepared the night before into a small saddlebag.

With considerable difficulty they managed to get out of the kitchen without the dogs, and hurried across to the stables. The sky was lighter now, and by the time they rode out of the yard it was almost dawn.

Alison realised right away that she need have no fears of Gavin's ability to manage the big black horse, for he rode competently and easily. Knowing they had a long day's riding, they conserved both their own energy and the horses' by keeping their reins light as they trotted over the plain.

Far in the distance lay the mountains they were heading for, blood-red now in the dawn.

'But they change colour through the day,' Alison said when Gavin remarked on this. 'I've seen them yellow, brown, green, and then blue, when it's nearly dusk.'

She had made sandwiches, and when they reached the bend of the river they stopped to have them.

'We should have a campfire, even a small one,' Gavin said. 'There's something nice about a campfire.'

'We'll make a fire later, when we cook the meat we have,' Alison agreed. 'I know what you mean, I like a campfire too. *Thirra-moulkra*, the Aborigines call it — the gathering round a campfire, a symbol of friendship. Jessie, the old Aboriginal woman who helps my mother in the house, used to tell Brian and me some of the old ideas and superstitions.'

They packed up then, and rode on, Gavin obviously interested in the things Jessie had told her.

'And the Dreamtime?' he asked. 'I've never been

able to grasp exactly what they mean by that. Is it the Great Unknown?'

Alison shook her head.

'No, it's more — the beginning of everything; it's a state they return to when life on earth is over. Jessie said the thing that comes nearest to it is when it's night, and the starlit skies are peopled with Aboriginal people going about their everyday affairs.'

She had never before told anyone what the old woman had told her, not even Brian. But somehow it was very easy to tell this big dark man riding along beside her, his eyes alight with interest.

There was no gradual rising towards Blue Rock Ridge; the plain stretched vast and flat, until suddenly the mountain range rose ahead of them, steep and often sheer. Blue Rock itself they reached along a fairly well-worn path, but halfway up they left the horses, lightly tethered, and went on on foot.

It was years since Alison had been here, and she had forgotten how cool it was, with the walls of black rock rising sheer on each side of the path, almost making a tunnel. And then the cave itself, not a big cave, but yet seeming to go right into the heart of the mountains. And the whistling.

It was only the wind, she knew that, she had always known that, and somehow she had thought that now that she was no longer a child she would no longer find it eerie and frightening. Involuntarily she shivered. And in the darkness of the cave Gavin's hand reached out and enclosed hers.

'We're going back out,' he said firmly.

And, keeping her hand in his, he led her towards the light at the mouth of the cave, and then out. The walls of sheer rock still rose steeply beside them, but even here, where the sun could never penetrate, it was warm again. And she could no longer hear the eerie whistling.

'Sit down,' Gavin ordered, and, all at once unable to argue, Alison sat down on a handy boulder.

'Why didn't you tell me you didn't like it in the cave?' he asked now, quite gently, sitting down beside her.

'It seems so stupid,' Alison said after a moment, embarrassed, and not wanting to say any more.

And then, seeing the real concern on Gavin's face, she knew she could go on.

'I've never liked going in the cave,' she admitted. 'But Brian did, and somehow, the more I hated it, the more I made myself pretend it didn't bother me.' She looked at him. 'It's only the wind, you know.'

'I know,' he agreed. And then, taking her by surprise, he said, 'So you used to be pretty good at facing up to things, even if you didn't like them?'

She knew it was pointless to pretend that she didn't know what he meant.

'Remember, you said no excess baggage,' she said.

'I know I did, but I think we need to take a good look at some of that excess baggage.' He took both her hands in his. 'Alison, why won't you face up to the truth of how you really feel about Steve Winter?'

She turned her head away, but he kept her hands imprisoned in his.

'You didn't love him, and he didn't love you. Oh, you were fond of each other, I'll grant you that, but that isn't love, Alison.'

That day in Edinburgh—and it seemed now so long ago, so far away—Morag had said much the same, Alison remembered. What was it she had said to Morag? Something about Steve and her not being the sort of people to be madly in love, about them being sensible and practical people.

Perhaps that was true, she thought now, painfully. Perhaps she had looked on what had really been no more than a good friendship as love. One thing was for sure — she had never, in Steve's arms, felt the way she did when Gavin Cameron kissed her.

How foolish, and how ridiculous, she told herself firmly. What do I really mean to this man, anyway? If it weren't for his precious sister, would he be here with me now, would he be looking at me like this? He said he would do anything to see that Tessa wasn't hurt, and perhaps this is for her.

It was a reasonable thought, a fair assumption — but she was dismayed at how hurtful she found it.

'It's none of your business how I feel about Steve,' she said abruptly.

'Oh, yes, it is,' Gavin returned.

'Because you're afraid he'll come to his senses about your sister?' she said scornfully — and unwisely, she knew, as his eyes grew dark with anger.

She turned away then, and went ahead of him down the steep path, stumbling once on a loose rock, but ignoring Gavin when he called to her to be careful. She was breathless when she reached the clearing where the horses were tethered, and when he joined her in the shade of a tree he was breathless too.

Breathless and angry, she realised as he looked down at her, unsmiling.

'For a girl with some intelligence,' he said abruptly, 'you can be mighty dim sometimes.'

And then, as he looked down at her, she saw the anger leave his dark eyes, leave his face.

'Let go, Alison,' he said, not quite steadily. 'Let go, and give yourself a chance. Give us a chance.'

'Us?' she repeated, unable to hide how much this disturbed her.

'You know damned well what I mean!' he said, impatient now. 'Heavens, woman, are you determined to go on fighting this? Don't go all coy—you know as well as I do how we feel about each other.'

He was very close to her. Alison backed away a little, but the tree behind her stopped her.

'Now wait a minute,' she said quickly. 'If you're into facing up to things and being honest, then I'll admit that—that there's undoubtedly a kind of attraction, but it's nothing more than that. A physical attraction, that's all. I'm not denying that.'

Even under the shade of the tree she could feel the heat of the sun burning through the thin cotton of her shirt. And she could feel the uneven thudding of her heart as the big dark doctor looked down at her.

'I'm glad about that,' he said softly, not quite steadily. 'All right, then, let's work on that for starters.'

His hands on her shoulders seemed to burn even more than the heat of the day.

'Now wait a minute,' Alison protested. 'I don't want any fireworks.'

His hands moved, drawing her close to him. 'I can't guarantee that,' he murmured. And then, his lips warm against hers, he said slowly, almost sleepily, 'Personally, I'm all for a few fireworks in my life!'

And he kissed her.

Now, alone in the silence of the outback, it seemed to Alison that the only reality in the world was this man, his arms around her, his lips on hers.

Everything she had said, everything she had thought, meant nothing against the inevitable way her body responded to his.

Later—much later—when somehow, instead of standing under the tree, they were lying on the rough grass underneath it, she felt Gavin move away, and she opened her eyes.

Gently but firmly he took his encircling arms away from her and sat up. Alison, conscious now of her rumpled hair, her flushed cheeks, sat up too. And she knew, as she looked at Gavin, that if he hadn't stopped she certainly wouldn't have. What she didn't know, she thought, was whether she was grateful or sorry about this.

'A bit old-fashioned, in this day and age,' he said, not quite steadily, 'but I find I have some principles.'

He reached out and took her hand. Without thinking, she moved away.

'Don't you believe me?' he asked. 'Don't you trust me?'

'I don't trust myself,' Alison told him honestly.

There was a moment's astonished silence, then Gavin threw his dark head back and laughed.

'Oh, Alison, I've been waiting all my life to meet a girl like you!' And then, the laughter gone, and his eyes very dark, he said, 'Not just a girl like you. You — just you, Alison.'

Alison turned her head away.

'Don't say things like that, Gavin,' she said, and her own voice was less than steady. 'Please don't.'

Not unless you mean it.

She was shocked at the clarity of this thought, unexpected, unwelcome — and unbelievably disturbing.

She stood up.

'If we're going to light a fire and cook our meat, we'd better get started,' she told him. 'We have a long ride back, remember.'

Gavin stood up too.

'We must have our fire,' he said. 'Our *thirra-*

moulkra, our symbol of friendship. If you won't accept anything else, you have to accept that.'

And later, over the flames of the small fire, he smiled at her.

'Friends, Alison?' he asked her.

'Friends,' she agreed.

It was a moment, and a closeness, that she was to remember later, when so much had changed between them.

Neither of them said anything more then, but it seemed to Alison that they had reached an unspoken agreement, and from them on everything between them was casual and light-hearted. They cooked their chops and sausage, and ate them with the home-made farm bread and coffee from the flask. And then, scrupulously, Gavin made sure that the fire was completely dead, that there were no embers that could be caught by the wind and could start a bush fire.

Then they untethered the horses and began the long ride back. Already the searing heat of the afternoon had eased, and Gavin pointed to a bank of clouds on the horizon.

'Looks as if we might get that rain,' he said.

'I wouldn't be too sure,' Alison replied. 'Dad was saying the clouds come up nearly every day, and everyone's hopes rise, and then they wake the next morning and the sky's clear again. We're lucky at Blue Rock Ridge — our dams are in a good catchment area, and they're not too low, but plenty of other farmers will be in real trouble if the rains don't come soon.'

They were halfway home, heading towards the river, when suddenly both horses whinnied and stopped, their ears pricked in alarm. The next moment there was a high-pitched, ear-splitting scream. Alison recognised it immediately—the piercing blast of a wild horse challenging all other horses.

'There he is,' Gavin whispered.

There he stood, silhouetted against a distant hill of red sandstone. He was looking back over his shoulder, head high, long mane whipping in the wind, and he looked gigantic, every line of him wild and savage.

Again he issued his shrill challenge, and both Alison and Gavin needed every bit of their strength to control their own horses.

It seemed an eternity before the wild horse, with another scream of challenge, turned and ran away, up the riverbed. And Alison, watching, had the strangest and most foolish longing for him to go free, never to be caught.

'He was like a demon horse,' she said, when they had managed to quieten their own horses. She patted the chestnut's neck. 'All mine wanted was to turn and run, but I think yours would have fought.'

'And if he had, the wild horse would have been the winner,' Gavin said soberly. 'At least we can tell your father and Brian where we saw him: it does give them a lead.'

Alison hesitated.

'Yes, of course we can,' she said carefully.

Gavin looked at her.

'We have to say we saw him,' he pointed out, and the unexpected gentleness of his voice, the unlooked-for understanding of her reluctance, unnerved her.

'It's ridiculous for me to want him to go free,' she said, and tried to smile. 'I'm a rancher's daughter, I know very well he can't be allowed to go on doing damage, killing other horses. But wasn't he magnificent, standing there, screaming his challenge?'

'Wild and free, which he should be,' Gavin said.

He looked down at her. And in a strange way she felt even closer to him in this moment of complete agreement than she had when she was in his arms.

'Yes,' she said at last, soberly, 'we'll have to say we saw him.'

Jim Parr was grateful to be told, when they got back, and said he and Brian would try to track the horse down the next day.

'Yes, I'm sure he's a magnificent animal,' he agreed, when Alison described him, 'but the station next door lost some of its brood mares — the stallion rounded them up and just led them away. I don't want that happening to ours. Now, come on and eat; your mother's convinced you must be starving.'

It had been a long and tiring day, but in spite of that Alison could see that the big doctor looked so much more relaxed than he had when they came.

She said that to him the next day, as they waved goodbye and set off for Namboola Creek and the hospital.

'I do have this tendency to look on myself as being able to keep going,' Gavin admitted, and smiled. 'Invincible, superman, that sort of thing. But I admit that I really needed the break.' He glanced at her. 'You needed it too, Alison. And I'd guess you're as stubborn as I am about admitting it.'

Alison opened her mouth to deny this, and then she thought that perhaps a discussion of whether or not she was stubborn could lead them to dangerous ground.

By common — and unspoken — agreement they kept off all dangerous ground on the drive back. They talked about the station, and the horses, about how Jim and Mary Parr had built up the station and their stock, about Brian and Meg and baby Ruth. About Gavin's memories of his childhood visits to his grandparents' station. They didn't talk about the wild stallion, and Alison was grateful for that. Seeing him had meant too much to both of them. She was certain of that, and that certainty in itself was disturbing.

It was only when Gavin drew up in the hospital grounds that Alison could see that he wasn't prepared to keep off the dangerous ground entirely.

He switched off the engine and looked down at her.

'Don't close your mind, Alison,' he said quietly. 'Be honest with yourself.' For a moment his hand closed over hers. 'And remember that *thirra-moulkra*,' he said.

Oh, yes, I'll remember that, Alison thought, as she left him. I'll remember our campfire, our symbol of friendship.

And then, unbidden, there was the memory of how she had felt in Gavin's arms, of her realisation that if he hadn't drawn back she wouldn't have been able to.

Symbol of friendship? Much more than that, she realised, shaken. Or was it? Perhaps it was no more than proximity, and this undoubted physical attraction. He was there, and he had made her see that she hadn't ever really loved Steve, that she wasn't heartbroken at losing him. Yes, she thought, he was there, and I was glad to turn to him.

And then, from somewhere deep inside herself, there was a question. If that was all it was, why did she find it so distressing, this doubt she couldn't get rid of, this questioning about his real motives?

Because this was what she kept coming back to. Was Gavin's real purpose to make quite certain she did nothing to hurt his sister, to come between Tessa and Steve?

* * *

Although she had only been away for a few days, it seemed to Alison that it had been longer, and it was a little while before the familiar hospital routine claimed her again, before she lost the slight feeling of disorientation.

But two surprisingly busy days on her maternity ward, with four deliveries in that time, and two of them happening when the doctor was unable to be reached in time, made the time on the station seem a little like a dream.

Young Molly, with Alison supervising, did one of the deliveries, and she was thrilled when the young mother decided to call her new baby girl after the nurse who had delivered her.

'I did do my deliveries to get midder,' she said to Alison one afternoon, when it was visiting time, there was a pleasant buzz of conversation in the ward, and for once all four babies were asleep at the same time. 'But this was different, somehow. I actually feel, after this, that I'd manage on my own if you weren't here, and if the doctor wasn't here.'

She put down her mug of coffee and picked up her knitting.

'A matinée jacket for Beth's baby,' she said, a little shyly. 'I've never been much good at knitting, but I thought I'd try this time. Well, I guess we're all looking forward to this one. We were all a bit thrown at first, but the thought of the baby, and seeing how much Beth wants it — now she's real keen too.'

And then, her bright young face shadowed, she said, 'At least, as long as Beth is all right. I'm just so glad you went to see her that day, and got her to tell you about the baby, and to see the doctor. She says he's keeping a pretty close check on her — he's got her convinced that she does need to rest, and to put her feet up, and I do think she looks a bit better already.'

Alison took the clinic book from the desk.

'I know she'll be seeing Dr Cameron regularly,' she said, turning the pages, 'but she should still come to the antenatal clinic next week — be a good chance for her to meet some of the other people.'

The antenatal clinic was always, for her, less interesting than the mother and baby postnatal, because she enjoyed seeing the progress 'her' babies were making. But certainly just as important, she knew, and already she'd seen that Gavin always managed to be there, no matter how busy the rest of the hospital was.

The following week she was glad to see Beth Garrett waiting with three other young women. And when each patient had had her blood-pressure taken, the foetal heartbeat checked, and the other samples taken, she was pleased to see that Beth didn't hurry away, but sat having a cup of tea and comparing notes with the other young women.

'Rick said he'd look after things this afternoon,' Beth said, when she left. 'Bye, Dr Cameron — see you next week. Bye, Ali — Sister Parr, Nurse Barton.'

And so he should, Alison thought, for she had already come to the conclusion that, pleasant and likeable as Rick Garrett was, he certainly didn't pull his weight as far as the work of the hotel was concerned. Still, the new baby on the way, and Beth's health problems, did seem to have made a difference.

Gavin thought so too.

'I'd say Beth looks better already,' he commented, when all the patients had gone. 'Can't say for certain, of course, until these blood samples come back from Charleville, but those dark circles under her eyes have gone, and her blood-pressure is normal.' He sighed. 'I am, of course, worried about Beth herself,' he said soberly. 'But even if we can keep the pregnancy going until the foetus is viable, we're a long way from home and dry. There could be intra-uterine growth retardation, we could have foetal death due to placental dysfunction.'

Alison had been thinking about this too.

'And anoxia during labour, as well,' she said. 'And even if we get Beth through all that, there's an increased danger of neonatal death, because the baby's very likely to be pre-term.'

They looked at each other. And then, with an effort Gavin smiled.

'But we're going to do our darnedest, you and I,' he said quietly, 'to see that none of these things happen, to see that Beth has her baby, and that they're both all right.' He stood up. 'I'd better reassure young Molly,' he said.

Alison followed him.

'Nicest ward in the hospital, this,' he commented, after he had talked to Molly about her sister. 'I always enjoy coming here.' And after a slight pause he added, 'To see the mothers and babies, of course. Don't you feel the same, Sister Parr?'

There was warm laughter in his dark eyes as he looked at Alison, and she was all too conscious of the young nurse's eyes, wide and interested, on her as she replied.

'Of course, Dr Cameron,' she said demurely. 'That's why we like working here, isn't it, Nurse Barton?'

The doctor handed his empty coffee-cup back to Molly. 'Thanks, Nurse,' he said.

When he had gone, Molly took the cups to the small sink and rinsed them. And then, very casually, she said didn't Alison think the doctor seemed a lot more relaxed and friendly these days?

Alison said, untruthfully, that she hadn't really thought about it, but, now that Molly mentioned it, perhaps he did.

But she knew very well that there was no doubt about the difference in the relationship between herself and Gavin. He was always correctly professional, but somehow the memory of the time they had shared out at her home, their friendship pact over the small campfire, the unforgettable moment when they had seen the wild stallion — all these things added a new and a warm dimension for their friendship.

But, in spite of knowing and admitting that, she couldn't help feeling an immediate reluctance when he asked her, quite casually, if she'd come out for dinner with him the next night.

'I know you're off, and since the only place we can go is the hotel, and it's only five minutes from the hospital, I can be called even more quickly than from my house,' he said firmly, forestalling any objections she might raise. 'And I could bet anything that even if the food in the hotel isn't exactly *haute cuisine* it's got to be a darned sight better than the food at the nurses' home!'

Alison had to smile at that.

'You're not wrong,' she admitted. 'But —'

'No buts,' Gavin said firmly.

'I was just going to say — is it such a good idea, in a place the size of Namboola Creek?' Alison asked. 'People do talk, you know.'

Gavin dark eyebrows lifted.

'So?' he said. 'Let them talk. I'd bet anything half the town already knows, anyway, that I spent a weekend at your folks' station.'

'That's different,' Alison said weakly.

A little desperately, she looked from the duty-room out into the ward, where Molly was just finishing a bedpan round.

'Molly will be back any minute,' she said.

'So we might as well get this settled,' Gavin said equably. 'You really are an argumentative, stubborn woman, Alison. I'm not going to rape you, seduce you, or ask you to marry me, at least not this time. I only want to take you out for dinner!'

'I don't see that you'd managed to do any of those in the dining-room of the hotel,' Alison returned. She smiled. 'Sorry, Gavin, I'd like to have dinner with you.'

And he was quite right, she thought remorsefully, after he had gone. Somehow, with him, she did tend to be stubborn and argumentative. It had become a habit.

It was only because she so rarely now did anything on her evenings off that she took a fair bit of trouble with her appearance the next night, she told herself as she hesitated between the white cotton dress that did a lot for her skin, golden again from the off-duty hours spent sunbathing, and the turquoise one that did a lot for her grey eyes and brought out the hint of russet in her hair.

She decided on the turquoise, and as she brushed her hair she was glad she hadn't got around to having it cut.

'Nice — very nice,' Gavin said appreciatively, when they met — Alison having drawn the line at allowing him to pick her up at the nurses' home. He smiled down at her. 'You look different, and you sure do smell different.'

Alison coloured, glad she had used some of the precious French perfume she'd bought in the duty-free shop at Heathrow as she was leaving.

'I don't think Chanel goes too well with disinfectant,' she said.

'Probably not,' Gavin agreed. 'Let's have a drink before we have dinner.'

There was a small ladies' bar, and Rick Garrett came through from the public bar to serve them. Beth, he said, was through in the dining-room.

'But she's only keeping an eye on things,' he said quickly. 'By this time of night she should be sitting down. Right, Doc?'

'Right,' Gavin agreed. 'You see that she behaves herself, Rick.' He turned to Alison. 'Cheers,' he said, and lifted his beer. Alison lifted her small glass of sherry.

'I hear there's been some rain,' he said. 'Picked it up when I was on the radio calls.'

'I heard too,' Alison said. 'But my dad says they're still waiting—clouds still piling up, and then disappearing. But one thing he said I was to tell you—they tracked the wild horse, and they spent a couple of days going after him, but he got away. Last they saw of him, he was heading north for the plain the far side of the next station—Dad says he'd be happier if they'd managed to shoot him.'

'I'm glad he got away,' Gavin said. 'I hope he has the sense to stay right out in the flats, away from anyone's property, or anyone's brood mares. I kind of like to think of him free.'

'So do I,' Alison admitted. 'As a farmer's daughter, I shouldn't be sentimental, but he really was magnificent, wasn't he?'

'Something I'll never forget,' Gavin agreed. And Alison knew that what she would never forget was the closeness there had been between Gavin and herself, as they watched the wild stallion, as they shared their longing for him to be free.

And suddenly the thought was there, as if it had been

slowly taking shape. Free. Just as she was free of Steve, free of the past.

It was a strange thought, a disturbing thought. But did this big dark man have the same thought?

He was looking at her, his dark eyes questioning. All at once uncomfortable, Alison was only too glad to see Beth, and to say hello to her as she came towards them, to say that their table was ready.

'I suppose there are marvellous restaurants in Edinburgh?' he asked her, when they were in the dining-room.

'Yes, there are,' Alison replied. 'But I wasn't in many of them, Gavin — you don't do that kind of thing on a nurse's salary, you know.'

He leaned across the table.

'You're not going to tell me that there wasn't some young Lochinvar desperate to come out of the west and — well, and take you out for the evening?' he asked her.

Alison shook her head, smiling.

'Not too many,' she said. 'And young folks in Britain are very much into equality — going Dutch for an evening out. But yes, there were some good places to eat — one in the old Grassmarket, right below the Castle; it used to be an old dungeon. It had marvellous food, and a terrific atmosphere.'

'Some day I'm going to see Edinburgh for myself,' Gavin said. His eyes met hers, and she thought he was going to say something else. But he seemed to change his mind, and after a moment asked her instead how her roast lamb was.

'Not too inspired,' he said, when they had finished their stewed fruit and apples. 'We'll think of something different to do next time.'

Next time? For a moment Alison was about to

challenge him on this, but two things stopped her. First, the memory of him asking her why she always had to argue. And second — and very much more valid — the realisation that she had to admit she was enjoying this evening with Gavin, and she would enjoy seeing him again, meeting him like this, away from the hospital.

'Let's have coffee through in the lounge,' Gavin said, and they went out of the dining-room and along the passage. There was the usual hubbub of noise from the public bar, at the far end, but the lounge itself seemed fairly quiet.

But just inside the door Alison stopped. Because there, sitting at a small coffee-table beside the door to the veranda, were Steve Winter and Tessa Cameron. And it was too late to turn and go back, because Steve had seen them, and had risen to his feet — looking, Alison thought, more than a little awkward.

'You set this up!' she said to Gavin, her voice low.

'I didn't, as it happens,' he returned. 'But I'm not too surprised, I have to admit.' His hand was very firm on her elbow. 'Are you afraid to meet him?' he asked.

Alison lifted her chin.

'Afraid?' she repeated. 'No, of course I'm not.'

And then, with his hand still on her elbow, she walked over to Steve and the fair-haired girl beside him.

'Nice to see you, Steve,' she said clearly, coolly. 'And you, Tessa.'

Behind her, and so low that only she could hear, the doctor murmured, 'That's my girl!'

Oh, no, Alison thought. I am not your girl, Dr Gavin Cameron, not now or ever!

CHAPTER SEVEN

IF I have to do this, Alison thought, then I'll carry it off with an air!

'Fancy seeing you here,' she said, as she pulled out a chair, and sat down, determined to give neither Steve nor the doctor the chance to do that for her. 'Not that there are too many choices of places to go in Namboola Creek. Going in for a meal?'

Steve shook his head.

'No, we've already eaten; we just came along for a drink,' he said. 'Tessa made — what was it we had, Tessa?'

'Beef Stroganoff,' Tessa said. She flushed, and then, half awkwardly, half defiantly, she went on, 'I'm trying to get Steve to be a little more adventurous than sticking to steak or chops!'

Alison wasn't sure why she didn't just leave it. Perhaps, she thought later, it was just because she was angry at Gavin, angry and resentful.

'You're in for a struggle, Tessa,' she said sympathetically. 'On the stations in the outback, men don't think they've had a real meal unless it's steak or chops!'

'It was very good, I enjoyed it,' Steve said.

For a moment, Gavin's eyes met and held Alison's. Without a word, his message was clear: That's far enough. Just watch it.

He smiled across the table at his sister. 'I hope you kept some for me; your Stroganoff is one of my favourite meals.' And once again his eyes met Alison's.

All right, she returned silently. I just wanted you to

know you weren't getting away too easily with this meeting! But I'll back off now.

She turned to Steve and asked him if there had been any rain on the station.

'A little — just enough to lay the dust,' Steve replied. 'I hear they're still waiting at Blue Rock Ridge too. But that big dam of your dad's still has water — it'll be pretty crook for me if there isn't some soon. Hey, I hear you two saw the wild stallion. Brian and I met to sort out some fencing, beyond the river, and he was telling me. Seems as if he's off further north now, though.'

'I'm glad he got away,' Alison said. 'I know he could do a lot of damage, but he's a magnificent animal.'

But it was something she didn't want to talk about, she realised with surprise, that moment when she and Gavin had reined in their horses and looked across the plain at the wild stallion, his mane flying in the wind, issuing his fearless challenge. It was a moment that had been too personal, too intimate between Gavin and her, to be shared. And for a fleeting moment, as his eyes met hers, she had the strange certainty that he felt the same.

She turned to Tessa and asked her how her dancing and aerobics classes were going.

'Building up slowly,' Tessa said. 'But folks really do seem to appreciate the chance to do something like that.' She hesitated, and then said diffidently, 'Come along some time, Alison — try a class, see if you like it.'

Alison, on the point of refusing, changed her mind.

'I might do that,' she said. 'Where do you have your classes?'

'In the big front room of our house,' Tessa told her eagerly. 'We really didn't need such a big house, but this one beside the school was the only one available when Gavin got the job here, so we took it. I brought big wall-mirrors with me, and Gavin put up some barres for the ballet classes, and it does very nicely.'

They talked for a little while longer, the four of them. Alison was very conscious of a few curious glances from the other people in the room, and she was determined to show anyone who was interested that she was quite capable of having a civilised conversation with the man she had thought she would be marrying, and the girl he had chosen instead. Most of all, she knew very well, to show Gavin Cameron. But it was a relief when Gavin said he thought it was time they left.

As they left the hotel, he looked down at her.

'Thanks for saying you'd go along and try out a class with Tessa,' he said. He smiled. 'I could see you were having something of a struggle with yourself.'

'I'm not quite sure why I didn't just say no,' Alison admitted. 'She's easily hurt, that sister of yours; maybe I'm not as hard-hearted as I think I am — or as you think I am.'

He looked down at her.

'I don't think you're hard-hearted, Alison,' he said softly. And then, disconcertingly, he laughed. 'Quite a few other words I'd use to describe you, mind, but not hard-hearted!'

It shook Alison, this disturbing feeling of closeness, of intimacy, that this man could give her. She reminded herself that she was angry with him for knowing that they might meet Steve and Tessa at the hotel, for not warning her.

'I don't like being manipulated,' she said brusquely.

He stopped.

'I didn't mean to do that,' he said. 'But I do admit that I wanted to force you to be honest with yourself.'

'Let go,' he had said, when they had come out of the cave. And she had; she knew that in her heart. But it wasn't something she could say easily to this man. She turned away, not saying anything.

'You are one stubborn woman, Alison Parr,' Gavin said. 'I really don't know why I —— ' He stopped.

'Why you what?' Alison asked, knowing this wasn't wise.

In a moment they would be in the brightly lit grounds of the hospital. But now, under the big mulga tree outside the gate, it was quite dark.

'You know darned well what I was going to say,' he said, not quite steadily.

For a long time, he looked down at her. She was very conscious of his closeness, of his maleness, there in the warm darkness. And very conscious that one step, one movement, from either of them, was all that it needed.

'Goodnight, Alison,' Gavin said.

She did move then, but it was too late. He was gone.

And you'd think, she found herself thinking in the next few days, that were was nothing but a completely professional relationship between us!

Not that she wanted anything different, of course. Actually, it was very reassuring to know that, no matter what happened between Gavin and her personally, there would not be a problem about working together.

The results of Beth Garrett's tests came back from Charleville, and Gavin came along to the maternity ward to tell both Alison and Molly.

'So far, we're getting away with it,' he said, sitting on the edge of Alison's desk in the duty-room. 'Blood-pressure we'd already tested; we'll check it once a week. No protein in the urine test, and her potassium level is acceptable. No oedema, and if there is we'll treat it with a mild diuretic. Thanks, Molly.' He took the mug of coffee Molly held out to him. 'Try not to worry, girl,' he said to the young nurse, and Alison saw that the kindness in his voice made Molly have to brush her hand across her eyes. 'We'll watch all the way. Slightest sign of her blood-pressure rising, or an elevated blood urea level, and we'll have her in. Meanwhile, Beth's sticking to her low salt diet, the baby is growing, and every week gained gives the baby a chance.'

And Beth, Alison thought soberly, for she knew from Beth's files that, after the kidney damage with the last birth, renal failure was a very real possibility. She was glad that the doctor, right now, for Molly's sake, was concentrating on anything positive he could point out.

'Thanks, Dr Cameron, I feel better about things now,' Molly said, her freckled young face brightening. 'Time for a bedpan round — at least life is predictable just now!'

But a few days later their smooth and regular routine on the maternity ward had a dramatic change.

Alison was alone in the ward, because Molly Barton was having a late lunch-hour. She had just got all three of the current babies settled in their tiny cots, and all three mothers were making plans to meet regularly after they got home, when Gavin came striding in, his white coat flying.

'Can I talk to you, Sister Parr?' he said, and without waiting for her reply he went into the duty-room. Alison followed him. He had taken one of the files out of the antenatal filing cabinet and was studying it.

'Mrs Martin,' he said, without looking up. 'From Warby's. Cardiac problems.'

Alison didn't need to refer to the file.

'Baby's due in a month,' she said. 'And we're sending her through to Charleville next week, so that she can deliver through there.'

Gavin put the file down.

'Too late,' he said, and she could see that his brusqueness hid concern. 'She's in labour; her husband's bringing her in—looks as if there won't be time to get her through. So you'd better get ready for a delivery with cardiac complications.'

They went through to the tiny labour ward together, and then Gavin went off to check on any other drugs or equipment that might be necessary for a patient in labour with cardiac problems.

'I want Jean Butler on standby,' he said. 'She may need nitrous oxide and oxygen, and you and I are going to be pretty occupied.'

Half an hour later Alison heard the scream of tyres outside her ward, and hurried out to meet the stockman and his wife.

'You can wait here, Mr Martin,' she said, taking him into the small waiting-room. 'As soon as Dr Cameron has seen your wife, we'll let you know what's happening.'

She took the young woman through to the labour ward and helped her out of her clothes.

'I was supposed to go through to Charleville to have the baby, Sister,' Mrs Martin said, not quite steadily. 'Maybe there's still time, if they took me in the plane?'

'We'll see what Dr Cameron says,' Alison replied, knowing very well what Dr Cameron would say.

Five minutes later the doctor came in.

'Still in the first stage, Sister?' he asked, and Alison confirmed that.

Swiftly, expertly, he examined the young woman.

'Right,' he said cheerfully. 'Nurse Barton is making tea for your husband, he looks as if he could do with it, then he can come in and sit with you for a bit. I'm just going to give you this injection, and, when you've got that man of yours convinced that we can catch babies here just as well as they can in Charleville, Sister Parr and I will be back in.'

Back in the duty-room, he looked at Alison.

'I've been in touch with Hartley in Charleville,' he said. 'He's the cardiac fellow, he would have been looking after her. But there's no time — she's likely to go into second stage soon, and we can't risk sending her through. So this is what we're going to do. I've given her Diazepan to keep her calm — that man of hers isn't helping; he's a lot more jumpy than she is. If necessary, we'll give her morphine later. We've to avoid over-hydration, and use a slow pump to control the IV fluid intake. And watch for increased cyanosis, and a pulse over a hundred and ten. So you're going to be pretty busy.' He looked at his watch. 'I have to get back to the general ward,' he said. 'But send for me the moment she's in second stage.'

Alison went to the door with him.

'And if there's any problem about getting you right away?' she asked him, carefully keeping her voice calm and steady.

'There shouldn't be,' he assured her. 'I'll be right there. But just in case, here's what we'll be doing. She'll need continuous oxygen, and she must be allowed to take whatever position is most comfortable. She mustn't push, because that heart will never stand it. We'll shorten the perineal phase by doing an episi-otomy, and I'll use a vacuum extractor to do a low forceps delivery.'

He ran his hand through his thick dark hair.

'I don't like it,' he said, his voice low. 'Heck, I'm way out of my class with this; she needs a fellow like Hartley in charge.'

Alison put her hand on his arm.

'We haven't any choice, Gavin,' she said, and somehow it didn't matter that in the stress of this moment she hadn't said Dr Cameron. 'We'll do the best we can for her, and for the baby.'

He looked down at her, his eyes dark, questioning. And then, with difficulty, he smiled.

'Thanks, Alison,' he said. 'I needed that. Let's go and see how she's doing.'

Under the influence of the Diazepan, the young woman was much calmer, and this seemed to have helped her husband too. Gavin told them that Sister Parr would send for him as soon as it was necessary.

'Just keep your wife company, and do whatever Sister Parr tells you,' he told the stockman. 'She's pretty bossy, so I wouldn't argue with her if I were you!'

It was only half an hour before Alison sent Molly to tell Gavin that Mrs Martin was in second stage.

'I was hoping she'd hold out a bit longer,' Gavin said to Alison, his voice low, when he had examined the young woman. 'They're sending packed cells through, in case she needs a blood transfusion to avoid overloading the circulation. Hartley can't come himself, but his senior assistant is coming. Could be an hour till they get here, though. And without a monitor we just don't know what that heart is doing.'

With the theatre sister assisting as well, and the oxygen and nitrous oxide taking effect, Mrs Martin was very drowsy.

'As soon as the head's far enough down,' Gavin said, 'I'll do an episiotomy, and a low forceps delivery. Without being able to monitor her heart, I'm not prepared to take any risks.'

Alison had worked with him often enough now to anticipate what he wanted, and a little later, when the baby's head was far enough down, she handed him the instruments he needed for the episiotomy, and then the delivery. Gently, carefully, he applied the forceps to the baby's head and drew the squirming little bundle out.

Alison had just handed the tiny, red-faced baby girl to Molly when the young doctor from Charleville hurried in.

'Sounds as if you hardly need me,' he said, above the surprisingly loud crying of the baby.

'We need you,' Gavin said tersely. 'Your chief says this is the tricky time, when the retracted uterus returns blood to the general circulation. I'm mighty glad to see you here.'

The young doctor, scrubbed up, joined them at the table.

'As soon as the afterbirth is delivered, we'll give her ergometrine,' he said. 'Does less harm than severe blood loss.'

He had brought a portable monitor with him, and he set it up while Gavin did the necessary stitching.

'She's pretty stable now,' he said, his eyes on the monitor. 'And the baby sounds fine. Good job, Dr Cameron. How's the baby, Sister?'

'I've suctioned her, and her Apgar score is eight,' Alison told him.

'Pretty good, considering the delivery problems,' Gavin said. 'Now what?'

The young doctor looked at his watch.

'I'm taking her and the baby back with me,' he said. 'She still needs to be monitored, and the baby's a month early, and I know Dr Hartley will want to persuade this young woman to have a tubal litigation done. With a heart like hers, she shouldn't risk having any more. We were talking about the possibility of a bypass for her, before the pregnancy. I think it should be done as soon as possible—make sure she stays around to see this little one grow up.'

Molly appeared then with mugs of coffee.

'Just what I need,' the young doctor said. 'Want me to have a word with the father, before we get on our way?'

Gavin shook his head. 'I'll do that,' he said.

Alison, cleaning up her labour ward, saw him go through to the small waiting-room and sit down beside the waiting stockman. The door was open, and although she couldn't hear what Gavin was saying she saw him put his hand on the man's shoulder, and she saw the young father, after a moment, manage a smile.

A little later the two men were at the door.

'Let's give Ted a minute with his wife and his new daughter, before they're whisked away,' Gavin said. 'That all right with you, Sister?'

'Of course,' Alison replied. 'We've got your wife through here now, Mr Martin, until the ambulance comes to take her to the plane.'

She led him through to the ward, hoping he wouldn't be too alarmed at his wife's exhausted white face. But Mrs Martin managed a smile as she drew the blanket back from the baby's face.

'Glad we've got our girl?' she said softly.

'Too right I am,' the big fair-haired man said gruffly. 'Not that I'd have minded another boy, but—well, two wild ones like our two is enough!' He leaned forward, and kissed his wife's cheek. 'Look, girl, I'll be through to Charleville soon's I can get the boys organised. Mr Warby says it's OK for me to go. You look after yourself, now, and this little one.'

Half an hour later the ward was quiet again. The ambulance had taken the new mother, the baby, and the doctor out to the airstrip, to go to Charleville,

Gavin had gone back to the main part of the hospital, and the three mothers were ready for visiting time.

'That was a bit of excitement, wasn't it, Sister?' one of them said, wide-eyed. 'She going to be all right?'

'Yes, she should be,' Alison replied. She turned to Molly. 'I'm just going to take Mrs Martin's folder over to Dr Cameron's office; he wanted to complete it.'

With visiting hour approaching, she wasn't sure if Gavin would still be here, but she could leave the folder on his desk, she thought. The door of his office was slightly ajar, and she knocked and went in. Then she stopped.

Gavin was sitting at his desk, but he was fast asleep. His head was down on his bent arms, and his thick dark hair was untidy. His head was slightly turned to the side, and she could see the dark smudges of weariness under his eyes. It had been a long, hard day for him, and he had possibly been on call through the night too.

She stood looking at the sleeping man. The collar of his white coat was turned the wrong way, and she wanted to straighten it. And to smooth the thick dark hair back from his forehead.

It's just that I'm sorry for him, because he looks so tired, she told herself, sensibly, sternly.

She turned to go, but the man at the desk stirred.

'Alison?' he said, his voice blurred with weariness. 'Don't go away, girl.'

Slowly she turned back.

'Sorry—was I asleep?' Gavin muttered. He smiled, but he still looked tired.

Alison found herself remembering that other time she had seen him asleep, when she had been driving the hospital Land Rover, and he had fallen asleep with his head on her shoulder. And that morning at home, when she had gone to wake him.

There was a strange and a disturbing intimacy in the thought that she had been so close to this man. And warm colour rose in her cheeks at the memory of the way she had felt, so soon after both those times, in his arms.

'I brought you Mrs Martin's folder,' she said quickly, taken aback to realise the effort she had to make to sound brisk and professional.

'Thanks,' he said, taking it. 'Been quite a day, hasn't it?'

The collar of his white coat was still turned up, and once again she had this absurd and ridiculous desire to straighten it, and smooth the thick dark hair back from his forehead.

'It certainly has been quite a day,' she agreed.

'I didn't mean to fall asleep,' he said ruefully. 'Just sat down for a minute. I'd better ring Tessa and tell her I'm on my way now.' With his hand on the phone, he looked at her. 'You're off now too, surely? You wouldn't like to come with me — have something to eat with us?'

Alison wasn't sure, afterwards, whether it was the thought of him with so much consideration for his sister that he had to let her know when he was late, that made her react the way she did. Or perhaps it was more that she was thrown and disturbed by her own feelings, and her uncertainty about his. Because the questions were there, unspoken. Was he really interested in Alison Parr herself, or did he want to make quite sure he kept Alison Parr from winning Steve Winter back from his precious sister? And why should Alison Parr mind so much, so very much, if that was the bottom line?

'No, thanks,' she said abruptly. 'I wouldn't like to get there and find it was a cosy foursome, with Steve there too, and you once again set on showing me love's young dream!'

Gavin stood up. The sleepiness had gone, and so had the warmth in his lean brown face.

'I had no intention of doing that,' he returned, just as abruptly. 'Strange as it obviously seems to you, this was nothing more than a friendly invitation. I thought you looked tired, and perhaps a little lonely. As it happens, Steve's at home on the station, waiting and hoping for rain.' His eyes were very dark as he looked down at her. 'Because until the rains come he and Tessa can't think about making any wedding plans.'

Alison felt all the colour drain from her face. Not because of what he had said — after all, she shouldn't be surprised at that, and she knew now that she wasn't heartbroken, that what she had felt for Steve had never been love — but because of the old, cool hostility there was in Gavin's face.

'That bothers you?' he asked evenly. 'Yes, I can see it does. So you haven't given up? I might have known you'd hang in there; I might have known you weren't prepared to give Steve up that easily.'

The sheer unfairness of this took Alison's breath away. That, and the realisation that she had been in danger of letting herself think that their good working relationship, the time they had spent together away from work, the shared closeness that had slowly, steadily come to mean so much to her, had made him feel differently about her.

But it hadn't, she realised now, bleakly. Underneath it all he was still sure she would try to come between Steve and his sister. And equally sure he would not allow her to do that, by any means.

'You're wrong,' she said at last, with difficulty. 'I'm

not hanging on to Steve. As far as I'm concerned, all that's over.'

He looked down at her, his eyes dark, unsmiling.

Alison turned away, unable to say anything. But the doctor reached the door before her, and his hands on her shoulders stopped her.

'I'm sorry,' he said stiffly. 'There was no need for me to speak like that to you.'

Her own spurt of anger had gone, replaced by a deep and aching hurt.

'I'm sorry too,' she said, with difficulty. 'I shouldn't have jumped to conclusions the way I did.'

His hands were still on her shoulders. For a moment — an endless moment, she thought later — he looked down at her. She could feel her heart thudding unevenly. She could feel her lips parting, waiting for him, her arms ready to hold him close to her.

Abruptly he turned away.

Shocked at her own feelings, because they were in the hospital, and anyone could walk in at any time, and it was completely unprofessional, Alison turned away too.

'You won't change your mind about that invitation?' Gavin asked, without looking round.

'No, thank you,' she said, not quite steadily. 'I — I have to —'

'To wash your hair?' he asked, and unbelievably there was warm laughter in his voice. 'Oh, Alison, girl, what am I going to do with you?'

'Nothing at all,' Alison returned, recovering.

Now he turned round. 'I could think of quite a few possibilities,' he murmured.

She felt her cheeks flame.

'Goodnight, Dr Cameron,' she said.

'Goodnight, Sister Parr,' he replied.

But the warm teasing was still in his voice and, ridiculously, she was glad of that. Although she knew all too well that it could not erase the memory of the things he had said, the way he had looked at her.

From now on, she told herself, I will not let myself forget, ever, that Gavin Cameron will do anything to safeguard his sister's happiness.

The hot, still days went on and on, and each day the clouds built up into a solid bank, raising everyone's hopes of rain, and then disappearing through the long hot night.

The hospital was busy, but Alison's maternity ward was fairly quiet. The antenatal and postnatal clinics were well-attended, and Alison could see, as she assisted Gavin, that the young pregnant women, and the mothers with their babies, had grown to like and to trust the new doctor.

She said this to him one day when the last baby had been weighed, and admired, and sent off with his mother.

'Took a bit of time,' he said. 'Dr Mac had been around so long, everyone seemed to feel no one else could do the job. Did you see his postcard on the notice-board in the canteen? Looks as if he's enjoying his holiday with his sister in Darwin.'

He passed her the final folder, and Alison put it into the filing cabinet.

'When he gets back,' Gavin said casually, 'I was thinking of asking him to take over for a few days. When your mother was in with Meg and little Ruth last week, she said couldn't I get some time off, have another visit to Blue Rock Ridge. I said no chance till Dr Mac can take over. But maybe when he gets back?'

'Good idea,' Alison agreed, just as casually. 'My folks always like having visitors.'

'Oh, and your mother said that maybe you could get a few days off at the same time. She seems to feel both you and I could do with a break.'

His voice was innocent. Too innocent, Alison thought, and fleetingly she wondered what her mother was up to.

'I really don't know how Matron would feel about that,' she replied dismissively. 'We're always short-staffed.'

'Matron has very strong ideas about staff looking after themselves,' Gavin reminded her. 'Anyway, we can't do anything till Dr Mac comes back.'

It was a surprisingly tempting thought, Alison found, a break of a few days at home. With Gavin there too.

'I'd certainly like the chance to see more of my niece,' she said quickly, feeling she should justify any apparent agreement with this plan. 'She's a little pet, isn't she?'

He hadn't repeated his invitation to come and have something to eat with himself and his sister. Not that she really wanted anything more to do with Tessa Cameron than she had to, Alison told herself. Although she did feel a little guilty about not following up on the younger girl's invitation to come along to an aerobics class some time.

She had just come off duty late one afternoon, and was wondering if perhaps she should do that right now, and get it over with, when she heard the distant sound of the school bell.

Funny, she thought, at this time. But even as she thought it she knew why it was ringing. It must be a bush fire.

And the next moment she heard the small fire-engine

passing the hospital. She pulled on trousers and a T-shirt and ran across the yard to the hospital.

Gavin and Matron were coming out as she reached the door.

'I heard the bell,' Alison said breathlessly.

'Emergency call came over the radio just before that,' Gavin told her.

'Where is the fire?' Alison asked.

'Out at Glengyle,' the doctor told her. 'Seems the homestead is pretty much surrounded. And with the wind changing the way it has been, it could head for the town.' He turned to Matron. 'I'll take any staff I can,' he said decisively. 'We'll need a good first-aid station. You'll stay here in charge.'

'Molly can look after my ward,' Alison said. 'I'm ready to come.'

'Good girl,' Gavin said.

He strode across to the big hospital Land Rover and began checking the first-aid kits kept there. When Alison got back from letting Molly know what was happening, he was loading extra burn dressings.

Glengyle was only an hour out, but it was already dusk, and soon they could see the glow of the fire in the darkening sky. And as they drew nearer they could see the flames leaping over the dry bush. Alison knew that there would be men from every station here, fighting the bushfire, and as they drew up she could see that they were digging a fire-break, frantically trying to make a big enough band of bare brown earth so that there would be nothing for the fire to feed on.

'There's your dad,' Gavin said. 'And Brian.'

Alison had just seen her father and her brother, with the other men, foreheads glistening with sweat as they worked, silently and desperately.

The homestead seemed to be encircled with flames,

she saw with dismay, the hose from the small fire-engine, and the water from the hoses and buckets, hardly making any impression at all.

'First thing,' Gavin said, looking around, 'is to set up our first-aid station. We need somewhere near, but safe. Stay here, Alison.'

He was back in five minutes, and said briefly that the best place seemed to be the head drover's house. It was fortunately some distance from the homestead, and at the moment the wind was carrying the flames in the opposite direction. They had hardly opened up their boxes when the station owner's wife brought one of her children in, with a badly burned leg.

'Went back in for the dog, he did,' she said, as Alison got out the sterile box of tulle gauze soaked in burn dressing, and began to dress the boy's leg.

'Got your dog out, then, did you?' she asked, when she had finished.

The boy nodded. 'Her, and her pups too,' he said. 'She'd never have got all the pups out by herself, see.'

'Young fool!' his mother told him. 'Go and tell your dad he needs his hands looked at. No, I'd better tell him myself, he won't listen to anyone else.'

Five minutes later the station owner, a big, red-haired man, came in reluctantly.

'Plenty needing done other than this, but the wife insisted,' he grumbled.

'Let's see your hands,' Alison said.

Silently he held out raw, painful-looking hands. Alison dressed the burns, and then, knowing it was useless to try to keep him away from the fire-fighters, she found cotton gloves in the emergency box and covered the dressings.

Gavin, seeing that Alison and two of the other nurses could keep up with the dressings needing done, had gone to join the fire-fighters. But to Alison, glancing across to the encircled homestead, it seemed that no matter how hard the men worked the fire was no nearer being under control.

The long night wore on, with men coming in, one after another, to have their hands dressed. Their faces were blackened with the smoke, and, strong men as they all were, towards dawn she could see the exhaustion in their faces. Her brother Brian was one of them, and while she was dressing his burned hands he was able to assure her that their father was all right.

In the kitchen of the drover's cottage, a group of women were making coffee and sandwiches and taking them out to the men. Alison, straightening her weary back, saw a slight figure in jeans, fair hair tied back, hurrying back with empty mugs.

'Tessa?' she said, surprised.

There was a smear of black down one of Tessa's cheeks, and her shirt and jeans were smoke-blackened too. She stopped, and as she rubbed the back of her hand across her forehead another smear appeared.

'I didn't know you were here,' Alison said.

'I came over with Steve,' Tessa explained. 'We were just about first here.'

She looked exhausted, Alison thought.

'Take a rest,' she said. 'You're not —'

She had been going to say, You're not used to this kind of thing, but something in the other girl's face stopped her.

'I'm all right,' Tessa said shortly. 'I have to go, Alison — they need more coffee out there.'

Alison, turning to watch her go, saw that she was limping.

'Have you hurt your leg?' she asked.

Tessa turned round.

'No,' she said. And then, unwillingly, 'I had polio when I was a child. I sometimes limp when I'm tired, that's all.'

You don't know what my sister is capable of, Gavin had said to her once.

There was no time now to think of that, but Alison realised, even as she turned back to get more burn dressings ready, that Tessa must have worked very hard to overcome her disability, to learn and then to teach dancing.

And as the sky became lighter, and she could see as the women working in the kitchen went in and out, taking coffee and sandwiches to the weary, smoke-blackened line of fire-fighters, she was filled with unwilling admiration for this girl, so determined to help, to do her share with everyone else.

It was dawn when the battle to save the homestead was lost. Alison heard the final crash as the last timbers gave way. Beside her, the station owner's wife was still, and Alison turned to her. The woman lifted her head.

'Could have been worse,' she said steadily. 'We all got out safely, and they've saved the stock. I guess we'll just have to start all over again.'

Her son, the boy whose leg had been burned, was beside her. For a moment, the woman's work-roughened hand touched his head.

'Just as well you got all these pups out, son,' she said. 'I reckon we'll need every one of them to get going.'

Alison, her eyes blurred with tears, turned away.

A little later Gavin, his face as smoke-blackened as all the other men fighting the fire, came in.

'Sorry I left you lot on your own,' he said. 'It looked as if I could do more good out there. But we didn't manage to save the house.'

'No, but the barn's still standing, and the stock is safe in there,' Alison pointed out.

One of her father's stockmen came in then, his arm burned where a falling log had hit it in the last desperate attempt to save the homestead. Alison dressed his burn, and it was only when he had gone that she saw that Gavin was leaning against the wall, his eyes closed.

She moved towards him, and then saw his hands.

'Gavin — your hands!' she said, anxiety making her speak sharply. 'Come here and let me see them.'

For a moment she thought he was going to argue, then, wordlessly, he held out his hands to her.

'You won't be much use to anyone,' she told him, 'if you don't get these seen to right now.'

As she laid the tulle on the raw burns, carefully, gently, she saw him wince, and go white under the black smoke on his face. But he said nothing until she had finished.

'Thanks, Alison,' he said then. 'We're extending the fire-break around the barn. If the wind changes, there could be real trouble there.'

'Surely you're not —' she began, but he broke in.

'Yes, I am,' he assured her. With an effort he smiled. 'With your magnificent bandaging, and the government issue of gloves, I'm as good as new! See you later.'

With the dawn, the wind had become stronger, and the flames seemed to Alison to be burning even more fiercely. The fire had jumped over the fire-breaks in two places, and she could see the long line of men desperately trying to check it.

The next man to come in was Steve, with a burn on his arm. Alison was busy with another of the fire-fighters when he came in, and the older of the other two nurses put a dressing on it for him. She was just finishing when Tessa Cameron came in.

Alison saw her stop at the door, her eyes on Steve, her face, under the smears of smoke, white. She took a step towards him, involuntarily, and then stopped.

'What's this?' she said lightly. 'Trying to get out of doing any more work?'

'Too right I am,' Steve said. He held out his unbandaged arm to her, and she took his hand in both of hers.

'Are you all right, love?' she asked, not quite steadily.

'Sure, I'm fine,' Steve said. He touched the smear of dirt on her cheek. 'You look pretty awful,' he told her. 'I've never seen such a dirty face!'

It was as if there was no one else in the world for the two of them, Alison thought. She wanted to look away, but she couldn't.

And in that moment she knew that she had to accept the truth and the reality of this. She had begun to accept, that day when she and Gavin saw the wild stallion, that what she had felt for Steve was not and never had been love. But somehow, in some secret part of her heart, she had still thought there was nothing real, nothing lasting in what Steve felt for this girl from the city, this girl Alison had been so certain would never fit into outback life. But she knew now that she had been wrong in that too.

They do love each other, she thought, with clarity and with acceptance.

She thought of this girl working gallantly through the night, and was ashamed now of her stubborn certainty that Tessa would never make a wife for a station owner in the outback. Tessa would work hard at it, and she would succeed.

Because they belong together, she and Steve, Alison thought with certainty, in a way that Steve and I never did.

And with the acceptance in that thought there was something else.

Would there ever be, in her life, a man she would love and belong to so completely, a man who would love her, who would belong to her?

A man? Did she mean any man? she wondered, with painful honesty. Or did she mean Gavin Cameron?

CHAPTER EIGHT

THERE was no time then for Alison to dwell on this disturbing question, for there was a shout from outside.

'Wind's changed!'

Everyone in the cottage hurried outside — the nurses in the emergency first-aid station, the men having dressings done, Tessa, the women in the kitchen.

'The barn's all right,' someone said.

The fierce flames, almost within reach of the barn, and the livestock saved from the fire, were now whipped away in the opposite direction.

And there was silence among the fire-fighters, at the realisation that the bush fire was now heading for the town. Far enough away, at the moment, but everyone standing there knew how fast a fire like this could blaze its way across the dry plain.

'We could try a fire-break nearer the river,' Alison's father suggested. 'That would help. Say half of us do that, the other half try to stop it where there's a chance before it gets a hold.'

'Not much water left in the dam,' someone pointed out. 'And damn-all in the riverbed.'

But in spite of that there were no complaints, as the weary men picked up their buckets again.

Most of the injuries had happened in that last, desperate fight to save the homestead, and now there was a lull for the nurses, for the men digging the fire-break were, at least for the moment, in no danger from the flames, and the others had no choice but to conserve the little water there was, and let the fire take its course.

Because there was always the danger of the wind changing again, the last of the water had to be saved in case the cottages were in danger.

Tessa Cameron brought through coffee and sandwiches for the nurses, and it was only when Alison sat down that she realised every bone in her body was exhausted.

She had just finished the mug of coffee, when one of the other nurses, looking out through the open door, said, 'Is it the smoke that's making everything so dark?'

In a moment they were all outside, peering through the smoke-filled air at the sky. And above the smoke the clouds were dark and heavy, and covering the entire sky. But Alison knew very well that that could mean everything—or nothing.

There was a distant rumble of thunder. And then, slowly at first, it began to rain. Big drops of life-giving rain, falling now steadily and soakingly into the dams, into the dry riverbed. And on the flames of the bush fire.

It was the only thing, everyone knew, that could have stopped the fire. The pitifully inadequate water available, the desperate attempt to make another firebreak—without the rain, the bush fire would have blazed its way to Namboola Creek.

Soon the weary men trudged back, rain making small rivers through the black on their faces, but each one was able to smile. Except, Alison thought soberly, the people who had lost their home today.

'Don't worry about us, we'll be all right,' the station owner's wife said when Alison asked her what they would do. 'Happens to be an empty cottage; we'll move into that. And we'll rebuild. Tell you one thing, I'm holding out for a nice modern kitchen, with a stainless-steel sink!'

But Alison saw that just for a moment there were tears in her eyes as she looked at the smouldering ruin of her house.

'You'll bring Johnny through tomorrow, will you? Dr Cameron will want to have a look at that leg. And his dad's hands,' she said, as she gathered up what was left of the boxes of burn dressings.

Johnny, and his dad, and everyone else, she thought, as she carried the boxes over to the Land Rover. The busiest place in the whole hospital would be Casualty, with dressings to be changed, wounds to be inspected.

'Alison! Let's head back for the hospital; there's going to be plenty to do there.'

She turned round as Gavin appeared, his shirt soaked, his thick dark hair plastered to his head.

'Your hands are getting wet,' she said, absurdly.

He shrugged. 'So are everyone else's. You can change the dressings when we get back. Would you mind driving?'

He got in beside her, and the other two nurses sat in the seat behind them. The road, so dry and dusty when they came, was now treacherous and slippery. Near the river they saw that there were no more flames, only blackened bushes, smoking as the rain fell steadily on them.

'It was a near thing for the town,' Gavin said soberly. 'There's no way we could have stopped that fire without the rain. Once the wind changed, that was it.'

He glanced at her. 'You're quite a sight, Sister Parr,' he told her amiably.

'So are you,' she returned. And she was glad when one of the other nurses leaned forward then to join in, glad to be able to avoid any disturbing moment of intimacy with this man who could cause so much turmoil in her emotions.

The rain had been widespread, they heard when they got back to the hospital. Namboola Creek itself had had a good downpour, and when Alison phoned home her mother told her that Blue Rock Ridge had had its fair share too. And now that the leaden heat and dryness had broken there was a fair chance of more rain.

The next few days were a blur of work, and collapsing into bed, for with Alison's own ward still quiet she helped on Casualty, dressing burns, helping Gavin with the necessary debridement, changing dressings, checking for infection.

There was little time to think, and in some ways she was grateful for that. But she couldn't pretend that that moment of truth hadn't happened, and slowly, painfully, she had to face up to it.

She wished now that she had told Gavin that he was right about her feelings for Steve, right to see that she had mistaken friendship, affection, for love. And she wished that she could bring herself to tell him that she could see now that she had been wrong about Tessa, about the strength and trust of the way she and Steve felt about each other.

More than once she wanted to try, wanted to tell him all this. But each time the same thoughts, the same doubts, stopped her. Surely, she would think, lying awake in the warm stillness of the summer night, surely I'm right, and what I feel for Gavin Cameron is no more than a physical attraction? A strong attraction, yes, she would have to admit that, but nothing more than that.

And yet — and yet, if that was so, why did it disturb her, the thought that the only reason for his involvement with her was to keep the path smooth for Tessa to marry Steve?

And why did she keep remembering foolish things? That moment of closeness, when they had watched the wild stallion together. The relief they had shared, knowing he was free. And there was what Gavin had said to her that same day, outside the cave.

'I've been waiting all my life to meet a girl like you!' And then, as he looked down at her, 'Not just a girl like you. You — just you, Alison.'

Did he mean it? she found herself wondering now. And did she want him to mean it? No, of course she didn't, not when she was being realistic and clear-sighted about him.

It was a disturbing thought, and she told herself she was foolish even to give it house room. For surely, surely, she was right about this fireworks thing that happened between them? You could have the fire-works, the chemistry — whatever — and it didn't really mean anything, it was a physical attraction, nothing more. Pleasant, and — and exciting, yes, she'd have to admit that. But nothing more.

And of course it was only because she'd enjoyed the change of work that she was a little sorry when the pressure on Casualty eased and she went back to her own ward.

'Did you enjoy working with Dr Cameron?' Molly Barton asked very innocently.

'Yes, I did,' Alison replied. 'He's pretty impressive; he works quickly, but very thoroughly, and he never gives anyone the feeling that he's too busy for them.'

Molly raised her eyebrows. 'Funny,' she said, still innocently, 'I got the feeling once that you weren't too keen on him.'

Alison felt her cheeks grow warm. 'That was a — a personal thing,' she said. 'I've always respected him as a doctor.'

Molly nodded. 'Me too,' she agreed, the teasing

over. 'I just feel if anyone can let Beth have her baby it's Dr Cameron.'

With Gavin seeing Beth every week, and reading the riot act if she seemed overtired, or if her blood-pressure rose even slightly, there was a reasonable chance of her carrying the baby long enough to give it a fair start.

'I wanted Beth to go through to Charleville,' Gavin said to Alison one day when he had just seen Beth again. 'She's dead against the idea, unless there's real danger to her or to the baby. I know that if I insist she'll sit through there and worry about Rick and the kids, and the hotel, and that won't do her blood-pressure any good. So I guess we'll just have to keep checking, and maybe send for the Flying Doctor service to take her through.'

He finished writing in Beth Garrett's folder and put it down on the desk.

'I gather Dr Mac isn't coming back till after Christmas,' he said. 'So I won't be able to take your mother up on that invitation for a bit, unfortunately. But talking about Christmas — this dance in the school hall on Saturday — how about you and me going to it?' His voice was very casual, very light. But his eyes were resting on her face, dark and intent. 'I'd like it very much if you'd come with me, Alison,' he said quietly.

Alison hesitated. Was it wise, she couldn't help wondering, to let herself have any involvement at all with him, outside of the work they shared? When she had so many doubts about how he really felt, and about how she felt herself — surely they should keep their relationship completely professional, and nothing beyond that. And yet the way he was looking at her, his dark eyes intent on her face, it seemed that he really did want her to agree. And she knew that she wanted to go to the dance with him.

'I'd like that too,' she said.

Perhaps that night, she thought, she would be able to say to him that she could see now that Steve and Tessa really did belong together. And that that was all right with her.

Without making a big deal of it, she told herself hastily. And she hoped that he wouldn't either.

On Saturday evening she decided to wear her white dress for the dance. Her hair was longer now — she still hadn't got round to having it cut — and she had to pin it up every day for work. But for the dance she let it hang loose on her shoulders.

She stood in front of the one big mirror in the nurses' home, examining her reflection. The rinse had brought out the touch of russet in her hair, and she was glad she'd taken the time to use it today. And the white dress looked good now that she had a tan again.

You'll do, she told herself.

But Gavin's eyes said much more than that, although all he said was, 'Nice, very nice, girl.'

She had agreed, this time, that he should pick her up at the nurses' home, because Molly had assured her that the whole hospital knew that Sister Parr and Dr Cameron were going to the dance together. Gavin's Land Rover was parked at the door, waiting.

'I should have something a lot posher than this,' he said ruefully. And, without giving her time to object, he lifted her up in his arms and into the cab. And when she was seated he looked at her.

'I'm not much good at saying nice things, Alison,' he said, a little awkwardly.

'No,' she agreed sunnily, 'you're much better at the nasty things.'

He laughed, his dark head thrown back. 'Too right I

am,' he said. 'Anyway, I'm proud to be the one taking you to the dance tonight.'

As compliments go, she thought, it probably wasn't much, but she couldn't help feeling ridiculously pleased.

The school hall was only a short distance from the hospital, and Alison had a moment's surprising regret that they were there so quickly. It would be fun at the dance, with the hall all bright and decorated, and music, and dancing, but she had a foolish wish, right now, to hold on to this moment with just the two of them.

The school yard was already pretty full, but Gavin parked at the far side.

'Don't jump out, I'm coming to help you,' he said. 'You'll get your dress torn or dirty if you get out by yourself.'

He lifted her down, but this time he didn't let her go.

'Want me to issue a warning?' he murmured, his lips against her hair.

'A warning?' Alison repeated, not understanding.

'You know,' he said softly. 'Those fireworks you were talking about — don't people usually give warning of fireworks? Or perhaps you think there aren't going to be any. This time.'

His lips were warm and sweet on hers, and his arms held her so that she couldn't have got away even if she had tried. But she didn't try. She reached up to hold him closer, and there was only one moment when she could wonder, dazedly, how in all the world he could have thought there would be no fireworks.

It was a long time before they drew apart.

'I just wanted to set the tone for the evening,' Gavin said, not quite steadily. He touched her hair gently. 'I've made your hair untidy. Do you mind?'

'Do you think I do?' Alison countered.

In the warm dusk, he looked down at her. 'No,' he said consideringly. 'No, I don't think you do.'

He waited while she tidied her hair and put some more lipstick on. And while she took his handkerchief and made sure there was no lipstick on him.

'I don't mind everyone at the dance knowing I've just kissed you,' he told her.

'It wasn't your shade,' she said, lightly, happily.

And she thought, I really don't care. Fireworks, chemistry, physical attraction, whatever — I like it! And for the moment I'll settle for this.

Just before they reached the door Gavin stopped.

'I just want to warn you,' he said, and smiled, a slow, lazy smile that did very peculiar things to Alison, 'that I have no intention of taking you straight back to the nurses' home, like Cinderella, at midnight.'

'What did you have in mind?' she asked.

He shrugged. 'I thought we might drive down to the river — check how the water's flowing, after all the rain,' he suggested.

'We could do,' she agreed, and she smiled too.

What the heck? she thought, and suddenly all her questions and her doubts didn't seemn to matter as much as they had.

He took her hand. 'Come on — the music and the dancing are waiting for us!'

I should have said it now, she thought, told him now how I feel about Steve and Tessa. But it was too late, they were in the hall, and the music and the bright lights and the festive atmosphere engulfed them.

Perhaps it was because everyone was relieved about the good rains, or because it was almost Christmas, but there was no doubt that the people of Namboola Creek were all set to have a good time. Alison caught a glimpse of Steve and Tessa occasionally, through the crowds, but they were never close enough to do any more than wave. Once she found Gavin's eyes on her, as she glanced across at the other couple, and she was taken aback at the concern in his eyes. She wanted to tell him not to worry, tell him it was all right, but this wasn't the time or the place.

Later, she thought, perhaps when we go down to the river, I'll talk to him then.

And then, she and Steve were facing each other. For a moment she saw dismay on his face, and knew she had to take this chance to sort things out with him.

'Come on,' she said gaily, taking his hands in hers, 'and don't tell me dancing isn't your thing—I can see Tessa's managed to teach you quite a bit.'

They went on to the dance-floor in the middle of the less restrained dancing—this was a waltz, and there was no doubt, Alison found, that Tessa had indeed taught Steve something in the dancing line. But she could feel the tautness of his arms around her, and before the music changed she looked up at him.

'Steve, could we go outside?' she said. 'There's something I want to say to you.'

'Sure,' he said, after a moment. 'Sure, Alison.'

The school vegetable garden was at the back, and it was dark and quiet, once they were out of the path of light streaming from the open door.

It was hard, she thought, to find the right words.

'I haven't made things easy for you, I know that,' she said at last, slowly. And when he started to speak she shook her head. 'No—let me go on. Steve, I've been doing a lot of thinking. I should have said all this to you sooner, I know that. You and I—what we had was affection, friendship, but it wasn't love. I thought it was, and you thought it was, until you met Tessa.'

'When I told you I'd be waiting, I really thought that

was what I wanted,' Steve said then. 'You and me, getting married, settling down. Then I met Tessa, and I knew.' He stopped awkwardly.

'And I know too now,' Alison told him, her voice steady. 'I know that what you and Tessa have is real and lasting. And I want you to know that I'm not heartbroken. We've been friends all our lives, Steve, I — I hope we can be friends again.'

She looked up at him, and a rush of affection filled her.

'I want you to know,' she said, her voice low, 'that I wish you every happiness, you and Tessa.'

She stood on tiptoe and kissed him. And then, because of all the years they had known each other, all the hopes they had once had, she hugged him.

'Now go and tell Tessa what I said,' she told him. 'I'll be in in a minute.'

She watched him go back into the brightly lit hall. And then, as she was about to follow him, a figure stepped out from the darkness beside the door.

Gavin strode down the path to stand in front of her. It was dark, but not so dark that she couldn't see how very angry he was. Cold, and remote, and angry.

'You just can't let go, can you?' he said bitterly.

'You don't understand, Gavin,' Alison began, shaken by the cold fury on his face. 'I was just —— '

'I understand only too well,' he returned. 'I see now that you were just waiting for your chance. Keeping me quiet, accepting dates with me, letting me think —— ' He stopped. 'I should have known,' he said, his voice low. 'I should have known you wouldn't give up. But don't go thinking you've won Steve back. I know how he and Tessa feel about each other, and I bet right now he's cursing himself for one moment of weakness. I'm not even blaming him—the poor guy obviously didn't have a chance.'

Alison's shock had given way to a rising anger.

'I don't want to win Steve back,' she said. 'And I wasn't trying to. You haven't given me a chance to explain.'

The doctor shook his head.

'I don't need any explanations,' he said flatly. 'I'm not blind, and in spite of what you obviously believe I'm not a fool. I could see very well that you were making the moves. He didn't kiss you—you kissed him.'

'Yes, I did kiss him,' Alison replied, and in spite of all her resolution her voice was unsteady. 'But it was because——'

Once again he cut in.

'You don't owe me any explanations,' he said coldly. 'I'm not even worried about you hurting Tessa, because I know that nothing and no one can come between Steve and her. I'm just damned glad that I've had my eyes opened, that I can see you clearly.' He looked down at her. 'And if a kiss means as little as that to you, you won't mind this,' he grated.

His lips were hard and demanding, his arms held her ruthlessly. It was a kiss with passion, but with no warmth. And yet, his lips on hers, his body close to hers, Alison had to fight to retain control of herself.

He released her abruptly. And without another word he turned and strode back towards the lighted doorway, the noisy hall.

Alison didn't go back into the hall. She went round the side and out through all the parked cars and Land Rovers. And then, alone, she walked down the deserted street to the hospital.

There was no one around when she got into the

nurses' home, and she was grateful for that. She bathed, and went back to her room. But she didn't get into bed. She sat on the chair at the window, looking out, not seeing anything, seeing only Gavin's face, hearing only the contempt in his voice. And feeling, once again, the bruising coldness of his kiss.

By morning, when she had slept a little, that dull and dead feeling had gone, and she was once again angry with him. He hadn't given her a chance. He had seen her kiss Steve, but he hadn't heard what she had just said to him. And he didn't want to hear. Just as he had done at the start, he had believed the worst of her right away.

I don't care, Alison told herself defiantly, as she got ready for work. I don't need him in my life. I'm sorry we have to work together, but from now on the less I have to do with Dr Gavin Cameron the better!

And she could see, as the days went by, that the doctor had obviously come to the same decision. He was polite to her, and she was polite to him, and that was all. Molly Barton must have known that something had changed between them — Alison sometimes caught the young nurse's eyes on her, bewildered, concerned — but she said nothing, and Alison was grateful for that.

The old doctor was still away, so there was fortunately no chance of Gavin being able to leave the hospital, when Alison went home the following week for a few days. Brian was in town to collect some new fencing, and he picked her up.

'Are you sure you don't mind coming back to work over Christmas?' Matron asked when Alison went to say goodbye to her.

'I don't mind at all,' Alison assured her, for, pleasant as the thought of spending Christmas at home had been, somehow she felt she'd just as soon be working, and not having too much time to think. And working hard she certainly would be, for Matron was to take a week off over Christmas, leaving Alison in charge.

'Mum's disappointed you won't be home for Christmas,' Brian said, on the long drive back. 'She kind of thought after a couple of years away you'd do anything you could to swing it.'

'I could have,' Alison replied honestly, after a moment. 'But I'd just as soon be working, Brian.'

'Meg thought as much, when you said you could come home now instead of over Christmas,' her brother said after a moment. He glanced at her. 'Still feel bad about Steve?'

Alison shook her head.

'No, I don't, not any more.'

For a moment she thought he was going to say something more, but he changed his mind, and pointed out how much water there was in the river now.

In spite of her pleasure at coming home, Alison couldn't help feeling a little apprehensive, wondering what questions her mother would ask. But after one quick concerned glance, and a warm hug, Mary Parr seemed determined to leave any sharing of thoughts to Alison herself.

The first day there was no time, between visits to Meg, admiring and holding baby Ruth, visiting the stables, accepting the frenzied welcome from the dogs, and no opportunity, really, Alison told herself. But the next morning when she woke, and padded barefoot, in shorts and T-shirt, through to the kitchen, there was only her mother there.

'Coffee and toast, I suppose?' her mother said. 'Not even a boiled egg?'

'Tomorrow I'll have an egg,' Alison promised.

Her mother sat down at the table with her, very obviously, Alison knew, talking about the baby, about the hospital, about the rains. And all at once it was easier to speak than she had thought it would be, to say what she should have said weeks ago, so that her mother would worry less about her.

'Mum, you were right about Steve and Tessa,' she said slowly. 'Folk do have to follow their hearts. They love each other, those two, and I reckon she'll do her darnedest to make him a good wife.'

Silently, her mother poured more coffee.

'I did some thinking, once I admitted that to myself,' Alison went on, with some difficulty. 'And I realised that I wasn't heartbroken. I guess maybe what I felt for Steve wasn't the real thing.'

For a moment, her mother's hand covered her own.

'I used to worry, you know,' she said, 'about you and Steve. You'd never really known anyone else, either of you, and I was worried about you just drifting into marriage. And when you went away I couldn't help thinking that that would give you both a chance, maybe, to see things clearly.'

She carried the empty mugs to the sink.

'And I thought, too, that if you'd really loved him you wouldn't have wanted to go away. You'd never have left him.'

Gavin had said the same, Alison remembered.

But she wasn't prepared to think about Gavin, and she was grateful, if a little surprised, that her mother made no mention of the doctor, other than saying that perhaps after Dr Mac returned to Namboola Creek Gavin might manage to come and visit them again.

And to that Alison made no reply.

But it was ridiculous, she found herself thinking, in her few days at home, how often she found herself thinking about him. Just because he had spent these few days here with her, because they'd done a few things together, it was extremely foolish and pointless, she told herself, to allow him to cross her mind at all.

But that was more easily said than done. She would find herself standing on the veranda, looking across the vast plain, shimmering in the heat, towards the mountain range, blue in the distance, and she would remember that day she and Gavin had ridden over to the hills and gone into the cave. And her cheeks would grow hot as she remembered being in Gavin's arms, his lips on hers. A kiss so different from the way he had kissed her that last time, outside the school hall. So very different.

But perhaps even more than that she would find herself thinking of their campfire, and of Gavin repeating the Aborigine words after her — *thirra-moulkra* — gathering around a campfire. A symbol of friendship.

Friendship, she thought bitterly. Not much of a friendship, when he set himself up as judge and jury, without giving her, the prisoner, any chance to defend herself.

Anyway, why should she care? She'd been pretty clear-sighted about him from the start, she reminded herself. And she had certainly told herself, more than once, that this was only a physical attraction, nothing more. So really, when it had been such an — an unimportant, transient thing, there was no need to feel any real regret.

And I don't, she told herself determinedly.

But throughout her last day at home she was conscious, from time to time, of her mother's eyes resting on her, questioning, concerned.

'You sure you're all right, girl?' her mother asked as she was leaving.

'Yes, I'm fine,' Alison assured her. She hugged her

mother and her father. 'I'll ring on Christmas Day,' she
promised. 'Don't forget to hand out the presents I put
in the spare room, Mum.'

'We're not as well organised as you,' Meg said,
holding up baby Ruth for Alison to kiss. 'But Brian or
Dad will be through before next week, so you'll have
your parcels too.'

The baby's cheek was soft, and she smelled of baby
powder. Alison found herself wishing now that she was
to be at home for Christmas, giving little Ruth the
teddy-bear she had bought for her, exchanging presents
with the rest of the family.

Instead, she had chosen to work.

And I don't expect Gavin Cameron to spread much
in the way of Christmas spirit! she told herself.

Over the time Matron would be away, and Alison
taking over, she would have to be in the office, leaving
Molly in charge over in Maternity. Fortunately the
whole hospital was fairly quiet, and, barring emergencies, should stay that way while they were short-staffed.

As established now, Gavin was scrupulously polite to
her all the time, and she was the same.

'Would it be possible, Sister Parr, to send this order
form through to Charleville right away?'

'Certainly, Dr Cameron, I'll see that it goes off
immediately.'

Alison, hurrying over to the chemist's beside the
hotel during her lunch-hour on her second day in
charge, told herself that she was only too happy with
keeping their contact minimal and formal.

So absorbed was she in telling herself this that she
almost bumped into Beth Garrett, coming out of the
chemist as Alison hurried in.

'Sorry, Beth,' she said. 'Won't do you any good if I

knock you over, will it? I just realised I'm out of shampoo. How are you?'

'I'm fine,' Beth said quickly.

Too quickly, Alison thought, and she took off her sunglasses and looked at the young woman. There were dark shadows under Beth's eyes, and Alison didn't like the look of her skin.

She didn't want to alarm Beth, but at the same time all her professional training, allied to an instinct that experience had added to that, told her something was wrong.

'When do you see Dr Cameron again?' she asked casually.

'Day after tomorrow,' Beth told her. 'Everything was fine last week. Dr Cameron wants me to go through to Charleville in a couple of weeks; I could stay with Rick's sister. I'm not keen on leaving Rick and the kids, but — well, Rick thinks I should go.' She looked at her watch. 'I have to get back, Alison; we've an order coming in, and Rick's away.'

Alison collected her shampoo and walked back across to the hospital to Matron's office. She sat down at the desk and opened the drug book she had been about to check. But she kept thinking about Beth Garrett.

If Dr Mac had been here, she wouldn't have hesitated, she knew that. And if things had been as they once were between Gavin and her, she wouldn't have hesitated either. But now she wasn't keen to take any step that was even fractionally beyond their polite and purely professional relationship.

And yet —

She stood up, and without giving herself time to change her mind went along the corridor and knocked on the doctor's door.

'Come in,' he said, without looking up from the notes he was making.

'Dr Cameron,' Alison began, and he looked up then.

'Yes, Sister Parr?' Polite, attentive. And distant.

Alison lifted her chin. 'I don't want to be interfering,' she said, with some difficulty, 'but I met Beth Garrett just now. She's due to come to see you the day after tomorrow, she says, but I think she needs to be seen right away.'

Gavin looked steadily back at her, and she wouldn't allow herself to look away.

'If you think so, that's good enough for me,' he said, surprisingly. 'How are we going to go about it?'

We? He didn't really mean anything by that, she knew, and she didn't want him to.

The doctor's hand was already on the telephone.

'I don't think I can be anything but straight,' he said, answering his own question. 'All right with you?'

Alison nodded, and turned to go, but he signalled her to wait. She stood, a little awkwardly, while he dialled.

'Beth? Dr Cameron here. Look, Beth, Alison's just come in to my office. She thinks you should have your check-up today. No, right now.' There was a pause. 'Fine,' he said, 'I'll be in my office.'

He put the telephone down.

'She didn't even argue,' he said. 'So she can't be feeling too great.' He hesitated, but only for a moment. 'Are you busy right now?' he asked. 'Or could you come over with me to Maternity when Beth gets here? I think we should do a complete check-up.'

'Yes, I can come,' Alison replied. 'If anyone needs me, they'll know where to find me.'

Ten minutes later Gavin, with Beth beside him, looked into her office. Alison put her files away and joined them.

She was glad that Gavin was honest with his patients. Today, as he examined Beth, took her blood-pressure, looked at her swollen ankles, and checked the foetal heartbeat, he said very little. But when the tests were completed, and Beth had dressed again, he looked down at her.

'I think you know things aren't too good, Beth,' he said gently.

The young woman nodded.

'I tried to tell myself everything was fine,' she said, her voice low. 'But my ankles are bad, and I've got this headache.' She looked at Alison, and tried to smile. 'I was telling myself I'd be fine if I could just put my feet up for bit, but I could see you weren't too happy, Alison, and I was just thinking about that when the doctor phoned.'

'Your blood-pressure is up, there's oedema, and there's protein in your urine.' Now he smiled, but Alison could see that there was still a shadow in his dark eyes. 'But the good news is that the baby is fine. I reckon, although it's only due in five weeks, it's probably close to six pounds now. What do you think, Sister Parr?'

He had stood by while Alison too examined Beth, and now she nodded in agreement.

'Certainly not much under,' she said. 'Big enough to cope, Beth.'

Beth Garrett looked up at the doctor.

'So now what?' she asked.

'I'm going to radio to Charleville and ask them to send out the Flying Doctor plane for you,' he said. 'I'd like you through there as soon as possible, and if they agree with me they'll induce. Got your little bag ready?'

Beth nodded. 'I'll just go and collect it, and see to a couple of things.'

Once again Gavin's eyes met Alison's.

'I don't think so,' he said, his voice steady. 'I think you'll stay right here, put your feet up, and let us send someone over to collect your things. Can you arrange that, Sister Parr?'

'Yes, I'll send someone across,' she said.

Gavin stood up. 'I bet that kid sister of yours is wondering what's happening,' he said, and now his voice was more cheerful. 'I'll go and have a word with her.'

He was back in a few moments, Molly beside him. Her eyes were wide, and some of the colour had drained from her fresh young face, but she managed to smile.

'Always did like a bit of drama, didn't you?' she said to her sister. 'Tell you what, I'll ring Mum; she'll look after the kids, and keep an eye on things at the hotel till Rick gets back. Once I've done that, I'll see about getting you a cup of tea.'

Back in the duty-room, she turned to Alison.

'Is she going to be all right, Alison?' she asked unsteadily. 'And the baby?'

This was no time for anything but honesty, Alison knew.

'I hope so,' she replied. 'You know yourself, Molly, that there's a danger of renal failure if we let Beth go any longer. The baby has a fair chance now, and so does Beth, if we get things moving quickly. But we will. They'll send a plane, and she'll be in Charleville in a couple of hours.'

The young nurse had just come back from the main building, where she had gone to phone her mother, when Gavin hurried in. And Alison saw from his face that something was wrong.

'There's a storm over at Charleville,' he said tightly.

'Neither of the planes can take off. They say if it eases they could send one in a few hours. But I don't think we dare risk waiting that long.'

Alison waited while the doctor stood at the window, staring out. Then he turned round.

'We'll have to induce and deliver the baby here,' he said.

They both heard Molly's involuntary indrawn breath, and Gavin turned to her.

'Beth isn't in any danger right now, Molly,' he said quietly. 'But she could be, if we leave her for even a few hours. Now off you go and see that she gets a cup of tea; I'm sure she needs it, and after we set up the drip she can't have any liquid.'

When she had gone, he looked at Alison.

'We'll set up a Pitocin drip right away,' he said. 'That should get things moving. Can you be on standby to assist when she goes into labour, Alison?'

'Yes, of course,' Alison replied.

She went back to Matron's office and worked for almost two hours, but it wasn't easy to keep her mind off what was happening with Beth Garrett. Then she went back over to Maternity and into the small labour ward.

Beth's brown hair was spread out on the pillow, and her forehead was damp. Alison checked the drip, and moistened the young woman's lips with water. Rick Garrett had just arrived, and she told him he could sit with his wife, and keep on doing that. As she hurried back to her office she met Gavin, and stopped to speak to him.

'I'd hoped she'd be further on by now,' he said. 'Every minute she's in labour increases the possibility of eclampsia. If she does have a convulsion, both she and the baby are at high risk. I could give her a sedative, prophylactically, but I don't want to risk that.'

A sedative, Alison knew very well, could lessen the risk of eclampsia, but could bring its own risks of producing vomiting, diminished secretion of urine, and respiratory depression. With Beth's kidneys as they were, these were risks they dared not take.

'The foetal heartbeat is good and strong,' she reminded Gavin. 'The baby's in no problem.'

'Not yet,' Gavin said bleakly. 'Neither is Beth. Not yet.' With an effort, he smiled. 'Sorry,' he said. 'I'm not usually so gloomy. Let's be positive. See you soon in the labour ward!'

And half an hour later Molly came hurrying in to tell Alison that she was needed. Rick Garrett was sitting in the small waiting-room, as she hurried past.

'Shouldn't be long now, Rick,' Alison said, hoping she was right.

As she opened the door, Gavin turned round.

'See, Beth?' he said. 'I told you I only deliver babies when Sister Parr's around to keep me right. So you can get on with the job now.'

The young woman was in strong labour now, and as Alison and Gavin worked together, as they had become accustomed to doing, Alison was very conscious of Gavin's voice, deep and kind and reassuring, telling Beth what to do. And conscious, too, that they were a team, she and Gavin, working together.

'Good girl, Beth, that's it. One more, and that should do it.'

There was only a moment after the head crowned, and then, with another push from the girl on the bed, the little shoulders appeared, and then Gavin held the tiny body.

'A little girl, Beth, and she sounds good and strong!'

The incubator was ready, but Alison could see that the baby, tiny as she was, would be all right. She was crying healthily, her tiny red face outraged, her small fists flailing.

And Beth, too, would be all right. Oh, there would be tests done, she'd probably still have to be seen by the renal specialist in Charleville, but when Alison had cleaned her up Gavin took her blood-pressure again, and it had returned to normal.

'I think we can let Rick come and see his new daughter,' he said.

Alison went through to get Rick, and also Molly.

'Five minutes,' she told them. 'Then Beth needs to rest.'

Gavin followed her out of the room.

'Any chance of a cup of coffee?' he asked her. 'I could use it, and I'm sure you could too.'

In the duty-room, Alison switched the kettle on and got out two mugs. And while she was making the coffee she found herself thinking that all the time they were working together, bringing Beth Garrett's baby safely into the world, there had been no coolness between them, no distance.

Now, she supposed, it would return again, the careful politeness, the lack of closeness. She was shaken to realise how much that thought distressed her.

The coffee ready, she turned round. Gavin was sitting in the one armchair, and he was leaning back, his eyes closed. He was, she could see, exhausted. His thick dark hair was untidy, and he needed to shave.

She stood there looking at him, and all at once everything was very simple.

She loved him.

How could she have been so blind, when it was so simple? How could she have gone on trying to persuade

herself that what she felt for this man was no more than
a physical attraction?

But there was no happiness in the realisation.
Because it didn't really matter what she felt for him,
when she knew all too well how he felt about her.

CHAPTER NINE

ALISON stood there with the mug of coffee in her hand, and desolation in her heart.

'Coffee, Dr Cameron,' she said, and she knew she sounded abrupt, cool.

The doctor's dark eyes opened, and he sat up straight. She couldn't help wondering if he too was remembering the other times when she had seen him exhausted, and asleep. In the Land Rover, right at the start. And that other time, when he had been up all night, and she had found him asleep at his desk.

'Don't go away, girl,' he had said, that time.

But she knew that even if he had remembered there was no way he would give memories like that house room now.

'Thanks, Sister Parr,' he replied, equally coolly.

He had called her Alison just a little while ago, when they were working together to save Beth and her baby. But that had been no more than a moment of forgetfulness.

Suddenly she had to get out of the room, away from the pain of being with him, when she had just come to this shattering realisation of how she really felt about him.

'I'll be in Matron's office if you need me,' she said, and turned to go. But as she reached the door his voice stopped her.

'Sister Parr?'

Unwillingly, she turned round.

'Are you all right?' he asked brusquely. 'You look——'

'Yes, I'm all right,' Alison replied, with an effort. 'I'm fine.'

She left then, quickly, glad to find people waiting to see her in Matron's office—a deputation from the kitchen staff, Sister Butler, two young nurses wanting to switch their off-duty times, the hospital porter with a long and complicated second-hand account of problems with the big Land Rover. What was left of the day was so busy that there was no time to think, and by evening the storm that had kept the planes from taking off in Charleville hit Namboola Creek, and she was soaked just crossing the grounds to the nurses' home.

But by the time she had bathed, and had a late evening meal, she could no longer shut out her own thoughts.

How could she have been so blind? she wondered. Fireworks? Physical attraction? Oh, yes, that, but so much more. There was admiration, for a good and caring doctor, there was the tentative beginnings of what could have been a deep friendship, there was laughter shared, there was understanding. All that, and more, she had been too blind to see.

But none of that really mattered, she reminded herself. Because surely Gavin's reaction when he saw her with Steve, his immediate condemnation, proved what she had thought all along—that his only interest in her had been to keep her away from Steve.

If there had been anything more—if he had had any real feelings for her, surely he wouldn't have behaved the way he did? He hadn't given her a chance, he had been so sure he was right.

What was it he had said?

'You just can't let go, can you?'

The bitterness in his voice — she would never be able to forget that.

And the end result of it all was that they were as far away from each other as if she had still been in Edinburgh and he had still been in Canberra, and they had never met here in Namboola Creek.

The next day the Flying Doctor plane got through, and Beth and her baby were taken through to Charleville. Alison went to say goodbye to her and the baby.

'She's tiny, but she's perfect, isn't she?' Beth said proudly. 'Only needed to be in the incubator for a few hours, she did. Dr Cameron says baby girls born early are usually better fighters than baby boys.'

'Wouldn't you agree, Sister Parr?' the doctor said, coming into the room. And when Alison nodded, 'Have you told Sister what you're calling the baby, Beth?'

'Joy,' Beth said, a little shyly. 'We feel, Rick and I, that that's what she is to us. And we'd like her to be Joy Alison. We don't have godmothers in our church, but we'd appreciate it if you'd come and hold her when we have her christened. Would you mind?'

'Mind? I'm thrilled and honoured,' Alison said, not quite steadily.

'And you'll come too, please, Dr Cameron,' the young woman said. She smiled. 'Rick says there'll be a real good party afterwards.'

When the ambulance had gone, Molly turned to Gavin.

'What are they going to do for her in Charleville, Dr Cameron?' she asked.

'I don't know,' Gavin told her honestly. 'I feel she came through the pregnancy without further kidney damage, but they'll have to assess that. They may be able to control her renal dysfunction with drugs; I can't tell. I'm pretty sure they'll advise a tubal ligation, because she certainly couldn't risk another pregnancy. But all in all, Molly, I reckon she came through it better than I once dared to hope she would.'

Suddenly, it seemed to Alison, Christmas was upon them. The nurses decorated the wards, and the big artificial tree was brought out and set up in the entrance hall. Going out from her office one day, Alison overheard Gavin talking to Jean Butler.

'I've always had this idea,' he said, 'that just once I'd like to see what Christmas is like in Scotland.'

'I grew up in Yorkshire,' the theatre sister told him, 'and I'd have to agree with you. I sometimes think I'd give anything to see a bit of snow. Real snow, not this cotton-wool on the tree!' She looked round then, and saw Alison. 'You had a couple of Christmases in Scotland, Alison — that must have been pretty good.'

'It was great,' Alison agreed. 'But I kept thinking, This can't be Christmas, when it's so cold!'

'All depends what you're used to, I suppose,' Gavin said. And his voice was a little stiff, a little awkward now, because she was there, Alison realised with sadness. She left them, and went on to the general ward.

On Christmas Eve some of the choir members from the church came to sing carols. Alison, although her day's work was over, knew that Matron always attended this, so she stayed on and joined any of the staff who were available, in the big general ward. A little to her surprise, Gavin was there. He seemed to know, and enjoy, all the carols, she thought, watching him joining in 'O Little Town of Bethlehem', the printed hymn sheet in his hand, but obviously hardly needing to refer to it.

To her discomfiture, the doctor glanced across the

room then. Alison looked away, but not quickly enough, and she could feel her cheeks grow warm, for he must have seen that she was looking at him.

He stayed, as she did, for the tea and mince-pies always served to the carol-singers, but he took good care, Alison knew, to avoid being in any group she was in.

This wasn't the first Christmas she had spent working, and she found, the next day, as she had before, that there was a warm, festive feeling about the hospital that helped the occasional pangs of wishing she were at home. She phoned her folks, just after she'd had breakfast, knowing that, Christmas Day or not, they would be up early. Later, she promised herself, she would open the presents Brian had brought through a few days ago.

The small hospital itself was quiet, for, since they were short-staffed over this time, even minor and routine operations had been postponed until the next week. Gavin had said he would be at home all day, and able to be reached by phone, but Alison wasn't surprised when he appeared in the middle of the afternoon.

'Everything all right, Sister Parr?' he asked. And then, awkwardly, he wished her a merry Christmas. A wish she returned equally awkwardly.

'I'll do a quick round, since I'm here,' he said. He glanced at the files on the desk in Matron's office. 'You don't have to come with me if you're busy.'

Alison would have liked to accept that, but she knew very well that Matron certainly would have accompanied him, so she closed her files and went with him.

It didn't take long, because there were so few patients. Over in Maternity there was only one young mother and her baby, born two days before, and none due until the end of January.

'So we're not going to have a Christmas baby,' Gavin said, as he and Alison left Molly and walked back across to the main block. His Land Rover was parked at the door, but to Alison's surprise he didn't leave immediately. Instead, he stood with his keys in his hand, twirling them, looked at the distant mountains, and commented that it looked as if there might be some rain coming.

And then, as if he had made up his mind about something, he looked down at her.

'Tessa and Steve got engaged this morning,' he said abruptly. 'I — don't know if you knew.'

'No, I didn't know,' Alison replied, her voice steady. 'Please give them my congratulations and best wishes.'

Still he made no move to go.

'Tessa asked me to tell you,' he said stiffly, 'that they're having a party on Saturday night, and she would very much like it if you can come. She ——' He paused, and then tried again. 'She seems to feel that you and I know each other well enough for me just to ask you. I'm sorry about that.'

So he obviously had said nothing to his sister about what had happened between them the night of the dance, of the end to any relationship other than a professional one. Alison wasn't surprised at this, somehow, for she didn't think he would be able to speak easily about that. Just as she would not be able to.

'I'm sure Tessa will understand if you say no,' he said, after a moment.

It would be easier in so many ways, Alison knew that. Oh, not because of Tessa and Steve, but because of Gavin himself, because of the way things were between them. But — no, she thought, and unconsciously she lifted her chin. No, I will not have anyone saying or thinking I couldn't be there. Most of all, Dr Gavin Cameron himself!

'There's no need for that,' she said clearly. 'I'll be very pleased to come.'

Matron was back at work the day before the party, and Alison was glad to have plenty of time to get ready. Time to wash her hair and let it dry in the sunshine, time to have a leisurely, relaxing bath. Time to decide what to wear.

The sea-green dress, she thought, holding it in front of her. Somehow, after the night of the dance, she didn't feel like wearing the white dress again. And this was the one she always felt good in. Her hair was long enough now to be pinned on top of her head in a loose bunch of curls. Good, she thought. I look different.

Different from any other time Gavin Cameron has seen me, she finished the thought, a little unwillingly, for it was pointless and ridiculous to care at all what this man would think.

The big room where Tessa held her classes was bright and noisy and filled with people, and Alison was glad of that, glad to move from group to group, after she had congratulated Steve and Tessa, and admired the Victorian ring that had been Steve's grandmother's.

The ring that once could have been hers. But there were no regrets in that thought, not any more.

Just as he had done on Christmas Eve in the hospital, Gavin carefully avoided any group Alison was in. Once he turned round unexpectedly, and Alison felt her cheeks grown warm at the thought that he had probably seen that she was looking at him.

'Can I give you a hand?' she said to Tessa then, following her into the kitchen.

'Thanks,' Tessa replied with relief. She took a tray of

small sausage rolls out of the oven. 'Could you put these on one of these big trays? Thanks, that looks nice. Gosh, but people can eat, can't they?'

'They can,' Alison agreed.

'Alison,' Tessa said impulsively, 'have you and Gavin quarrelled or something?'

Alison, taken aback by the direct question, was unable to reply. The younger girl coloured.

'I'm sorry,' she said, 'it's none of my business, but I — I thought you were friends now; in fact I thought you'd come here together tonight. I didn't realise you'd be here on your own; I wouldn't have wanted that for you.'

'Oh, I know just about everyone here,' Alison replied lightly. 'Really, it's no problem, Tessa, coming on my own.'

But Tessa's blue eyes were still on her face, waiting for an answer to her question.

'Yes, you could say we've quarrelled, but it's nothing to worry about — we still work well together, and that's all that really matters,' she said, knowing her voice sounded determinedly bright. And then, because she didn't want this to go on any longer, discussing her relationship — or lack of it — with Gavin Cameron, she lifted the tray and said, even more brightly, that it looked as if there were some pretty hungry folks out there.

'Alison, I just wanted to —— ' Tessa began.

Alison pretended she hadn't heard.

Later, when she felt she could decently leave, because a few other people had already gone, she went to say goodbye and thank you to Tessa.

'I'm so glad you came, Alison,' Tessa said. She put her hand on Alison's arm. 'Thank you for saying what you did to Steve, the night of the dance. It meant a great deal to both of us that you'd said that.'

'I'm sorry it took me so long to reach that stage,' Alison replied, meaning it. And then, on an impulse, she said she would like to take Tessa up on her offer to come to one of her aerobics classes. 'Maybe next week?' she said, and Tessa's obvious pleasure made her glad she had said it.

The hospital was only five minutes away, and now, with the heat of the day gone, and a slight but welcome coolness in the summer night, she didn't mind the walk back. She was glad she had gone, but glad, too, that the evening was over.

Because one thing was now painfully clear to her. She was not going to find it possible to stay here in Namboola Creek, to work with Gavin, to live with this coolness and distance between them. To go on, day after day, seeing him look at her with cool hostility in his eyes — No, she thought bleakly, no, I can't take it.

She didn't want to leave — after all, it was her family, her home, Namboola Creek itself that had drawn her back, but she knew it would be impossible for her to stay.

'Alison!'

She turned, startled. Gavin caught up with her.

'I'm quite capable of walking back alone,' she told him. 'I suppose Tessa sent you to see that I got back safely.'

He looked down at her.

'No,' he said, 'Tessa didn't send me. And I have no doubts about your ability to look after yourself. No, I —'

Taken aback, she could see that he was at a loss for words.

'I saw you talking to Tessa, just before you left,' he

said abruptly. 'I asked her what you'd been talking about, and she told me. She told me just what you said to Steve, the night of the dance. I owe you an apology, Alison.'

'I tried to tell you, but you wouldn't listen,' she said, and to her horror her voice was less than steady. 'You didn't give me a chance to explain.'

'I know that,' he said, his voice low. 'That was unforgivable — but can you forgive me, Alison? Can we go back to where we were before that?'

No, she thought, no, Gavin, we can't do that. Because I didn't know then how I felt about you. I didn't know that I loved you. And I don't know now how I can love a man who showed so little trust in me.

He was waiting for her to reply, looking down at her in the moonlight.

'I don't know,' she said at last, honestly. 'I just don't know, Gavin.'

This time he was the one who took a long time to say anything more.

'Do you think we could at least try?' he asked her.

She thought of that moment when she had looked at him, and she had known that she loved him. In that moment of truth everything had seemed simple. But now it was less simple. Yes, she loved him, she was certain of that. But she didn't know how he really felt about her. Oh, there were the things he had said, there was the way he had looked at her, the way he had kissed her. But how did any of that stand up against the way he had judged and condemned her, without giving her a chance to explain, without giving her the benefit of any doubt at all?

'I don't know,' she said again, sadly.

Once, he had said to her, 'Let go, and give yourself a

chance. Give us a chance.' He was asking the same of her now.

'All right, we'll try,' she said, wondering even as she said it if this was something she would come to regret. Because the way she felt right now, no matter how hard they both tried, nothing would change the fact that he had judged her, that he hadn't given her any chance.

He smiled then, but the smile didn't reach his eyes.

'I'll keep you to that,' he said.

He walked back with her to the door of the nurses' home, but he didn't kiss her, or touch her. In the warm moonlight, he looked down at her.

'Goodnight, Alison,' he said quietly.

If Alison felt a caution and a reserve about this change, there was no doubt, she found in the next few days, that Gavin did as well. The formal politeness between them was gone, but there was no easiness yet. She wondered, with sadness, if there ever would be.

Matron was back, and Alison was relieved to be away from the office in the main building, next door to Gavin's own office, with an unavoidable number of chance meetings each day. Now that she was back in Maternity, he came over for his rounds, for the clinics, or when he was needed. Beyond that, she saw less of him, and she thought that that was just as well.

But when she came off duty a few days later, to her surprise he was waiting outside the nurses' home.

'I know you're off this afternoon,' he said, without any preamble. 'And I've just given myself the afternoon off too. How quickly can you change?' And then, before she could reply, he said, 'I'm sorry, I sound as if I'm giving you orders, and that's the last thing I want to do. Please, Alison, change into jeans or something and come out with me. Will you?'

'Where are we going?' she asked, a little breathlessly.

He shook his head, but he was smiling now, seeing that she was agreeing to come.

'You'll see,' he said.

Five minutes later, when she came out, changed into jeans and a T-shirt, he was in his Land Rover, waiting. She climbed up beside him, very conscious of one or two interested young nurses looking out of their windows.

He drove out of the town, and down to the river, all without saying a word. There he parked, and while Alison was getting out he opened the back of the Land Rover.

Mystified, Alison watched him take out some sticks, and then some small logs, and build a fire. Only when it was properly alight did he turn to her.

She was sitting on a fallen log, watching him, more than a little warily, she knew. He took both her hands in his and drew her to her feet and over to the fire.

'Surely you know what I'm trying to say, Alison?' he said to her. 'This is our *thirra-moulkra*, our symbol of friendship. I — couldn't think of any other way to make you realise how much this matters to me.'

Absurdly, she could feel her eyes fill with tears.

His hands tightened on hers.

'But I have to be honest with you,' he said, not quite steadily. 'It isn't just your friendship I want. You must know how much I love you.'

CHAPTER TEN

THERE was nothing he could have done, Alison thought later, more simple, or more right, than this.

She stood there beside the fire, with Gavin's hands holding hers, and she knew that all her foolish doubts had gone.

'All I want,' Gavin said quietly, 'is to make up for what I did. I should have given you a chance to explain. It was arrogant, unfeeling, judgemental — anything you want to call it.' His eyes were very dark as he looked down at her. 'I think I was so darned mad that I didn't know what I was doing! I'd been so sure we were getting somewhere, you and I, so sure that I might make a breakthrough and convince you that these fireworks just might have something more solid, more lasting than a Catherine wheel! And then there you were, kissing Steve.'

'And giving Tessa and him my blessing,' Alison said.

'And giving them your blessing,' Gavin agreed. He smiled. 'It was foolish, but I'd had a lot of hopes for that evening, and it just seemed to me ——' He stopped. 'I don't really think we need to go back on all that,' he said. 'I was angry, and I was stubborn, and that did enough damage.'

'I've been stubborn too,' Alison pointed out. 'It took me too long to admit to myself that you were right about Steve and Tessa, that they were right for each other. I wouldn't admit it until the day of the fire. I saw them together, I saw the way they looked at each other, and I knew that they were right for each other. And even before that I'd begun to see —— '

Gavin said nothing, but she knew he was waiting for her to go on.

'That I wasn't heartbroken,' she said steadily. 'That what Steve and I had was affection, it was habit, but it wasn't love.'

'I wish you'd told me that,' Gavin said.

'I wish I had too,' Alison replied. 'But I couldn't just come up to you in the hospital and say, Oh, by the way, I've realised that you were right, I didn't love Steve, now could I?'

Gavin smiled. 'No,' he admitted. 'No, you couldn't do that.'

'I was going to tell you, the night of the dance,' Alison said then. 'Later, I thought, when — when we were alone.'

He shook his head.

'You know,' he said, and smiled, 'we could go on with this long enough — if only, and why didn't we. But it really doesn't matter now. We've said the important things, maybe we'll say the rest, but right now I think we've done enough talking.'

'No,' Alison said steadily. 'There's something else I have to say, Gavin.' If she didn't say it now, it would always be there between them. So she said it, baldly. 'I thought you were — becoming involved with me to make sure things went smoothly for Tessa, to keep me from trying to get Steve back.'

His hands tightened on hers.

'I can't understand how you could think that,' he said, and the sheer disbelief in his voice cleared away the last of her doubts. 'How could you not see how I felt about you?'

He released her hands then, and went back to the

Land Rover, coming back in a moment with a rug which he spread out beside the fire.

'Sit down,' he said.

Alison sat down, and Gavin sat down beside her.

'I shouldn't give you orders,' he said. 'I know very well you don't take kindly to that.' There was warm teasing in his voice, and she loved it.

'What's your next order, Doctor?' she asked him demurely. 'We can see whether or not I take kindly to being given orders.'

Gavin lay back on the rug and looked up at the vast blue canopy above them.

'I had thought of trying to convince you that these fireworks have something pretty solid and lasting going for them,' he said to the sky.

Alison leaned over him and tickled his nose with a piece of grass.

'How did you think of going about that?' she asked him, a little unsteadily.

In one movement he took the grass from her and drew her down close to him.

'That,' he said, equally unsteadily, 'would depend on your co-operation, wouldn't it?'

His kiss was slow and sweet, and his lips were warm against hers. Then, as if the fire beside them had inflamed them, there was an urgent, searching demand that, this time, could not be refused.

Once, Alison stirred in Gavin's arms and murmured, 'What if someone comes?'

'They won't,' Gavin said, his lips close to hers. 'It's too hot, and everyone's still at work, and school isn't out.'

Just as well, was Alison's last conscious thought before everything else was blotted out, everything but a world that had narrowed down to herself, and the man whose arms she was in.

Later, much later, Gavin looked down at her.

'I think we should get married soon,' he said. 'Very soon.' He kissed the tip of her nose. 'Am I giving you orders again?'

'Maybe you are, but I happen to agree, so it's all right,' she told him.

'You haven't told me when that happened,' he said, and he lifted her left hand to his lips and kissed the palm. 'I don't really need to be convinced, but it's nice to know.'

'It was after you delivered Beth's baby,' Alison told him. 'I was making coffee, and you were sitting down. I was thinking that everything had been all right when we were working together, and that now we'd go back to being distant and polite again. Then I turned round, and you were sitting with your eyes closed. You were so tired, and you needed to shave, and I knew that I loved you.'

'Just like that?' Gavin said wonderingly.

'Just like that,' Alison agreed.

She leaned forward and kissed him. He released her hand and took her in his arms, but this time his kiss was tender, and gentle, a kiss with the promise of all the time ahead of them.

At last, with reluctance, they sat up, and then Alison folded the rug and put it back in the Land Rover, while Gavin stamped out the embers of the fire.

'Will you come back to the house with me?' he asked her. 'Tessa might be there, but it's a darned sight more private than the sitting-room of the nurses' home.'

'Anywhere is more private than that,' Alison assured him.

In the Land Rover, she looked at him.

'Are we going to tell Tessa?' she asked him.

'Not unless you want to,' Gavin said. 'I'd thought we shouldn't tell anyone until we see your folks and tell them.'

It would be nice, they decided, just to keep this to themselves for the moment. And so when Tessa came through to the kitchen after her last class Gavin just said he'd asked Alison to join them for supper, and was there enough.

'Sure,' Tessa said. 'It's a casserole, so it can easily stretch.'

They sat at the kitchen table, the three of them, companionably. Later Tessa insisted that she had some book-keeping to do, in her front-room studio, and she left Gavin and Alison watching television. Although neither of them, Alison was certain, could have told anyone what they had been watching.

She looked in to say goodnight to Tessa when she was leaving.

'I take it you two have made up any quarrel you had?' Tessa asked, polite interest in her voice, but laughter dancing in her blue eyes.

Gavin's arm was casually around Alison's shoulder. 'You could say that,' he agreed.

It was a fortnight before the old doctor came back to Namboola Creek, and could take over on Alison's weekend off, so that Gavin could go with her to Blue Rock Ridge.

'Was your mother surprised when you said I was coming too?' he asked, as they set off.

'Somehow, I don't think so,' Alison said. 'She just said that would be nice, and she'd have breakfast ready for us.'

It was very different, this journey to her home, from the last one. Then, they had been strangers. Cautious strangers, with so many conflicts between them. She would never have thought then that they would be coming here to tell her family that they were going to be married.

As they had before, they stopped at the river and had the coffee Alison had brought.

'You love it here, don't you?' Gavin said, as Alison stood beside the Land Rover, looking over the plain towards the distant blue mountains. 'We'll be near enough, in Namboola Creek, to visit pretty often.'

'I hadn't thought that far ahead,' Alison replied. She stood on tiptoe to kiss him, a brief butterfly kiss that brushed his lips. 'But I must admit that will be nice.'

'Oh, no,' he said, softly, and his hands caught hers. He kissed her very thoroughly, not letting her go until she was breathless. 'You're not getting away that lightly. With your mother's eagle eye on us, who knows when I'll get within an inch of you this weekend? Not to mention your father's eagle eye, come to think of it!'

When the homestead was in sight, though, he asked her, a little apprehensively, what she thought her parents would say.

'I don't know,' Alison admitted, but she remembered her mother saying that she had worried, sometimes, about Alison drifting into marriage with Steve. This, she thought, had certainly been no drifting. A rough voyage, with a few near shipwrecks on the way.

'What are you smiling at?' Gavin asked, and she told him. 'Not a bad way of describing our courtship,' he agreed. His hand covered hers. 'But look at it this way. If we hadn't had such a rough voyage, we wouldn't appreciate the harbour as much as we do!'

As it turned out, neither Alison's mother nor her father was surprised by their announcement.

'I wondered how long it would take the two of you to see something that was mighty plain to me,' Mary Parr said, when they were all sitting having tea on the veranda.

'And of course she told me, and then it was mighty plain to me too,' Jim Parr added solemnly.

Meg too, it seemed, had been waiting — 'For the two of you to come to your senses,' she said. She hugged Alison and then Gavin. 'I couldn't be happier.'

And that, Alison found to her wonder and joy, seemed to be the general feeling. Brian, Tessa, Matron, the old doctor, Beth and Rick Garrett. Everyone, it appeared, was happy for them — happy, and not at all surprised.

Suddenly, it seemed, the few short weeks had passed, and Alison was home at Blue Rock Ridge for their wedding. She and Gavin had driven through the night before, and Gavin was spending the night with Brian and Meg.

Alison woke early on her wedding-day.

It was hot and still, a perfect day in late summer, and when she looked out of the window she could see the trestle-tables set up under the shade of the mulga trees. Soon, she knew, her mother would be up, and supervising everything in the kitchen. Later in the morning the guests would begin to arrive — from Namboola Creek, from the sheep stations around.

Her dress was hanging up, and she touched the soft folds of it. They had decided, she and Gavin, that their wedding would be a simple one, and her dress was creamy silk, and the soft folds of the skirt reached just below her knees. Meg, in a blue dress, would be her only attendant. Later, her mother and Meg were to pick some flowers from the garden for her to carry.

She knew that her mother would be planning on bringing her breakfast in bed, but suddenly she wanted to be up and outside, part of this very special day. She slipped on shorts and a T-shirt and went outside, barefooted, on to the veranda. The dogs greeted her, and she patted them, and told them to be quiet.

Then, still barefoot, she went over to the stables. No one else was about, but she could hear, from Brian and Meg's cottage, the baby's demanding cries. So Meg would be getting up too, feeding the baby.

She went back into the house, into the silent kitchen, and made herself some coffee to take outside on to the veranda, where she would sit on the swing seat.

But the swing seat was already occupied.

'We can't go on meeting like this,' Gavin said, as she sat down beside him. 'Let's get married.'

'Yes, let's,' Alison agreed.

'How about today?' he asked, laughter in his dark eyes. 'Would that suit you?'

'I think I could fit that in,' Alison replied, laughing too.

He took the mug of coffee from her and set it down on the small table. Then he took her in his arms and kissed her.

'My mother will have a fit,' Alison said at last, breathlessly. 'You know she said last night we're not supposed to see each other until the wedding.'

'She'll never know,' Gavin assured her, and kissed her again.

'Oh, yes, she will,' Mary Parr said from the doorway. She was smiling. 'I might have known you two wouldn't be bothered with too many conventions. You might as well come in and have breakfast, Gavin, since you're here. Ready in ten minutes.'

When she had gone, Gavin looked down at Alison.

'I suppose you're going to be as bossy as your mother,' he said.

'I should think so,' Alison agreed. 'Do you mind?'

He stood up, and drew her to her feet.

'I suppose I'll learn to live with it,' he replied. He looked up at the clear and cloudless blue sky. 'Lovely day for a wedding,' he said softly.

A lovely day for the start of our life together, Alison thought, with wonder and with joy.

Gavin took her hand then, and they went into the house together.

LOVE ON CALL
4 FREE BOOKS AND 2 FREE GIFTS
FROM MILLS & BOON

Capture all the drama and emotion of a hectic medical world when you accept 4 Love on Call romances PLUS a cuddly teddy bear and a mystery gift - absolutely FREE and without obligation. And, if you choose, go on to enjoy 4 exciting Love on Call romances every month for only £1.80 each! Be sure to return the coupon below today to: Mills & Boon Reader Service, FREEPOST, PO Box 236, Croydon, Surrey CR9 9EL.

— — — — — — — **NO STAMP REQUIRED** — — — — — — —

YES! Please rush me 4 FREE Love on Call books and 2 FREE gifts! Please also reserve me a Reader Service subscription, which means I can look forward to receiving 4 brand new Love on Call books for only £7.20 every month, postage and packing FREE. If I choose not to subscribe, I shall write to you within 10 days and still keep my FREE books and gifts. I may cancel or suspend my subscription at any time. I am over 18 years. Please write in BLOCK CAPITALS.

Ms/Mrs/Miss/Mr _____ **EP63D**

Address _____

_____

Postcode _____ Signature _____

mps
MAILING
PREFERENCE
SERVICE